Stuck with You

Read more UNICORN and YETI books!

Sparkly New Friends
A Good Team
Friends Rock
Cheer Up
Fair and Square
Together

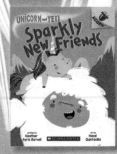

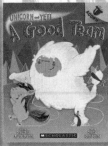

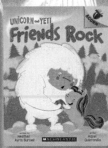

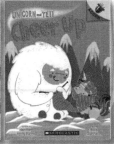

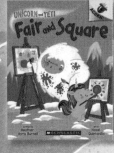

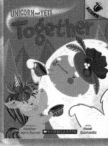

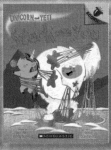

UNICORN and YETI

written by
Heather Ayris Burnell

art by
Hazel Quintanilla

SCHOLASTIC INC.

For my mom, who supplied me with plenty of bubble gum,
took me to the sticker store often, and let me roller-skate
as much as I wanted (which was a lot!). — HAB

For David, my magical best friend! — HQ

Text copyright © 2022 by Heather Ayris Burnell
Illustrations copyright © 2022 by Hazel Quintanilla

Library of Congress Cataloging-in-Publication Data

Names: Burnell, Heather Ayris, author. | Quintanilla, Hazel, 1982– illustrator.
Title: Stuck with you / by Heather Ayris Burnell ; illustrated by Hazel Quintanilla.
Description: First edition. | New York, NY : Acorn/Scholastic, Inc., 2022. |
Series: Unicorn and Yeti ; 7 | Audience: Ages 5–7. | Audience: Grades K–1. |
Summary: Unicorn and Yeti have fun together playing with stickers,
trying to roller-skate in the snow, and blowing bubbles.
Identifiers: LCCN 2021045950 (print) | ISBN 9781338826784 (paperback) |
ISBN 9781338826791 (library binding) |
Subjects: CYAC: Unicorns—Fiction. | Yeti—Fiction. | Friendship—Fiction. | Humorous stories. |
LCGFT: Humorous fiction.
Classification: LCC PZ7.B92855 St 2022 (print) | DDC [E]—dc23
LC record available at https://lccn.loc.gov/2021045950

10 9 8 7 6 5 4 3 2 1   22 23 24 25 26

Printed in China   62
First edition, December 2022

Edited by Katie Carella
Book design by Sarah Dvojack

Table of Contents

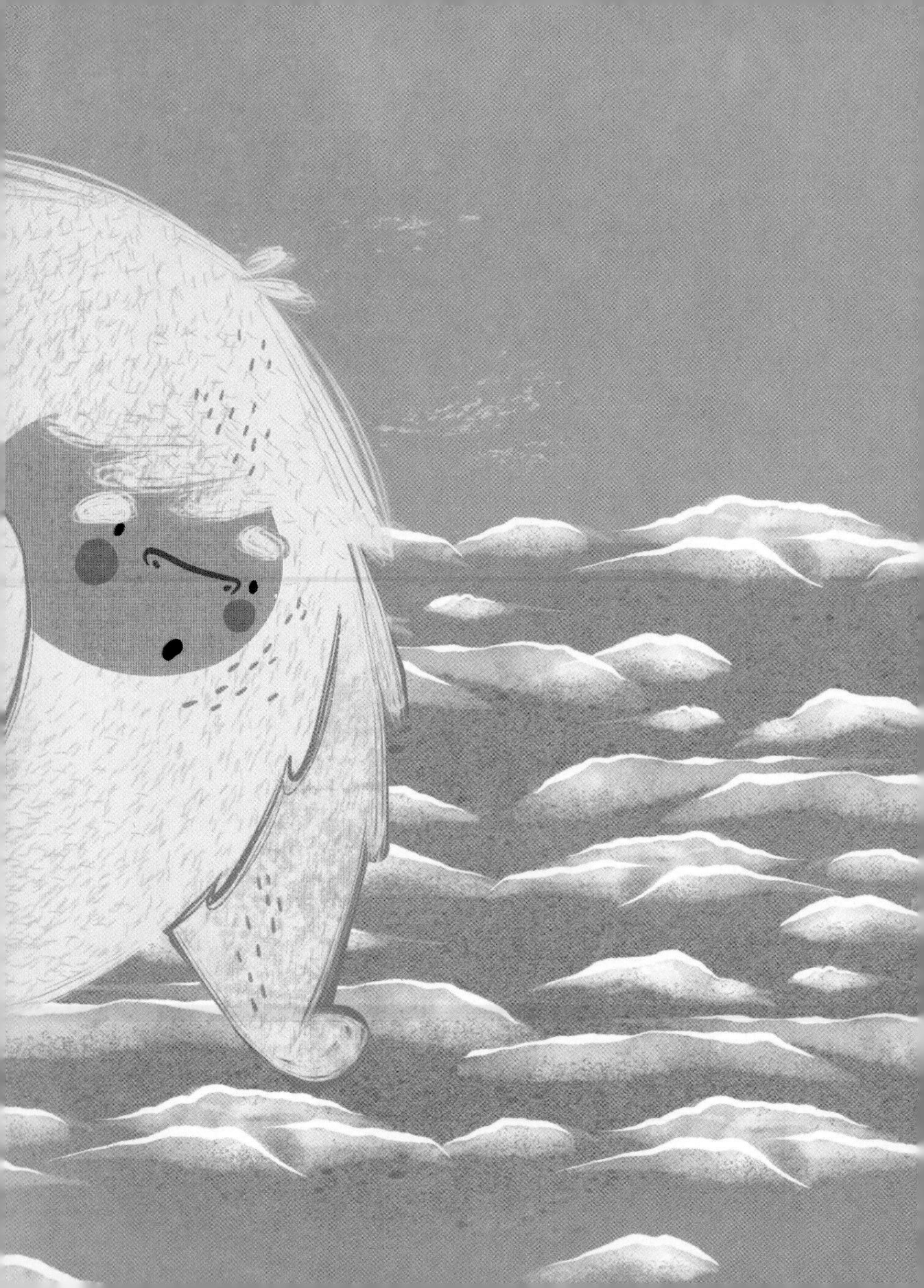

Stick! Stick! Stick!

Unicorn opened a book.

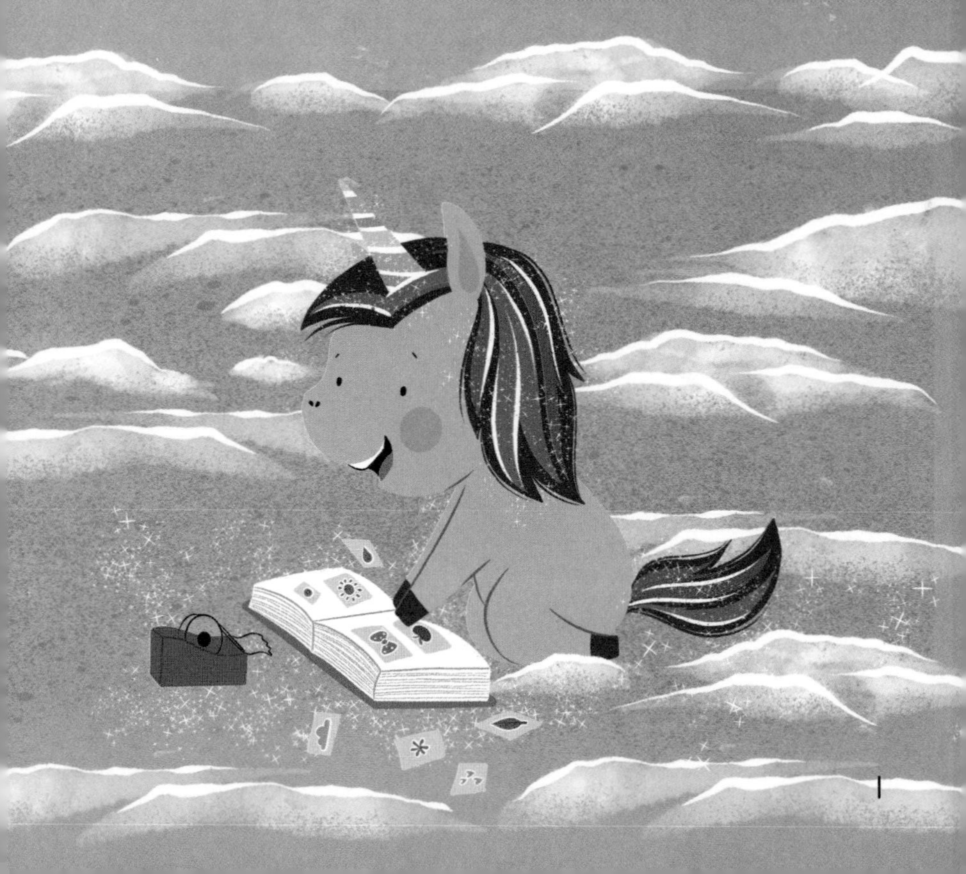

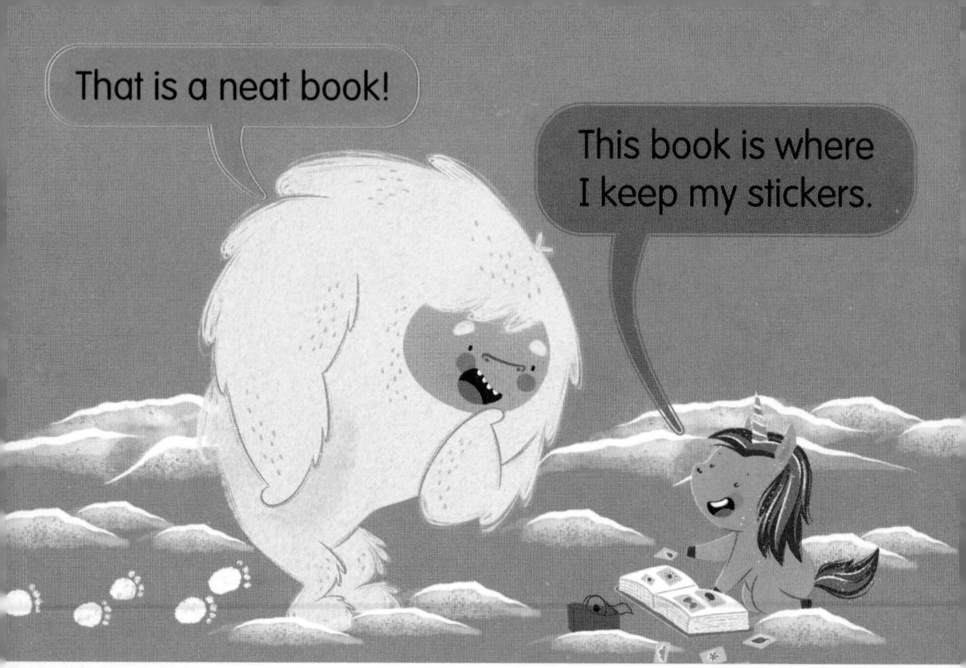
That is a neat book!
This book is where I keep my stickers.

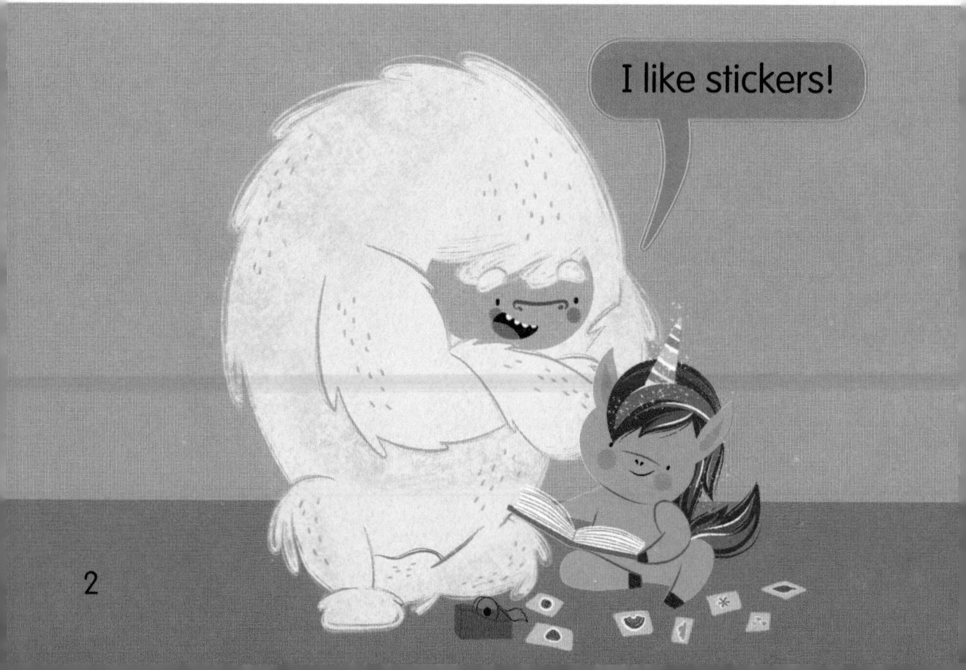
I like stickers!

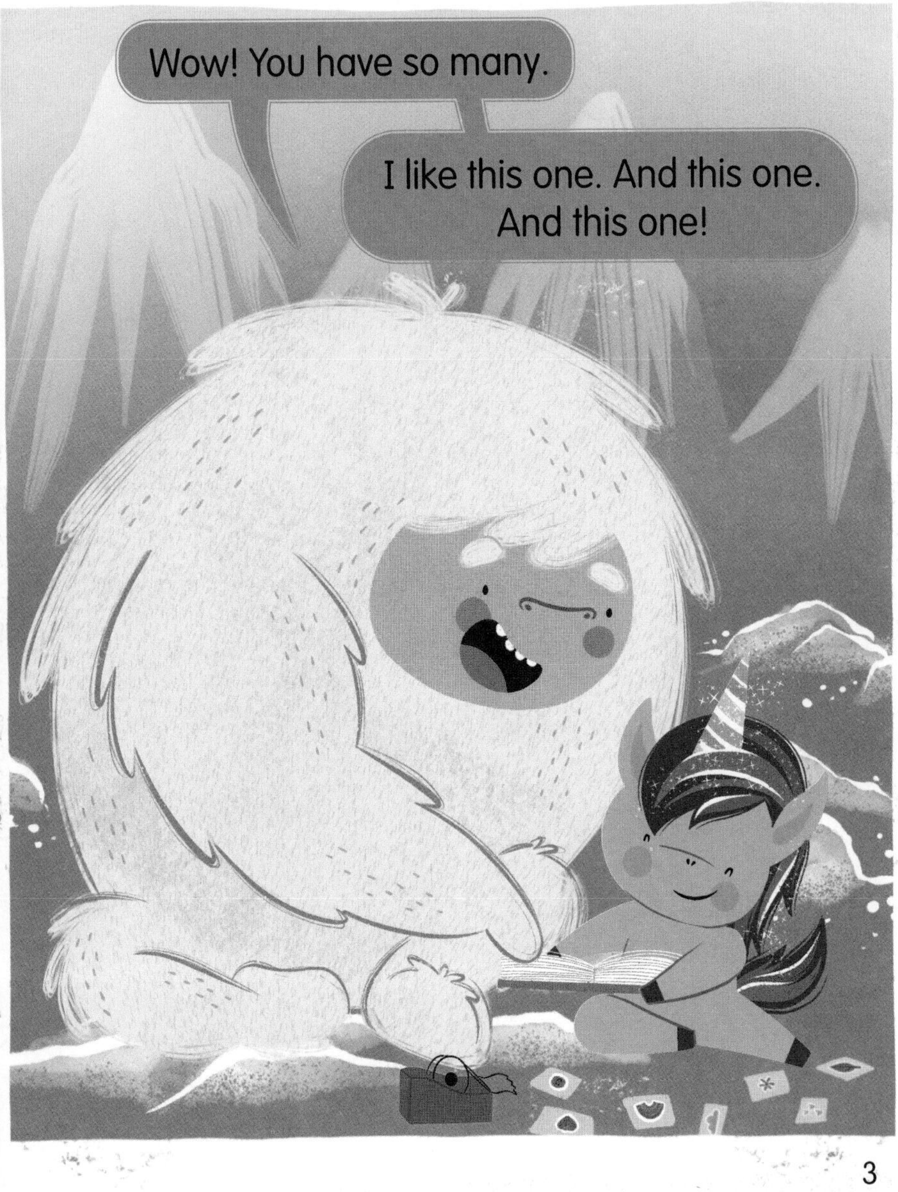
Wow! You have so many.
I like this one. And this one. And this one!

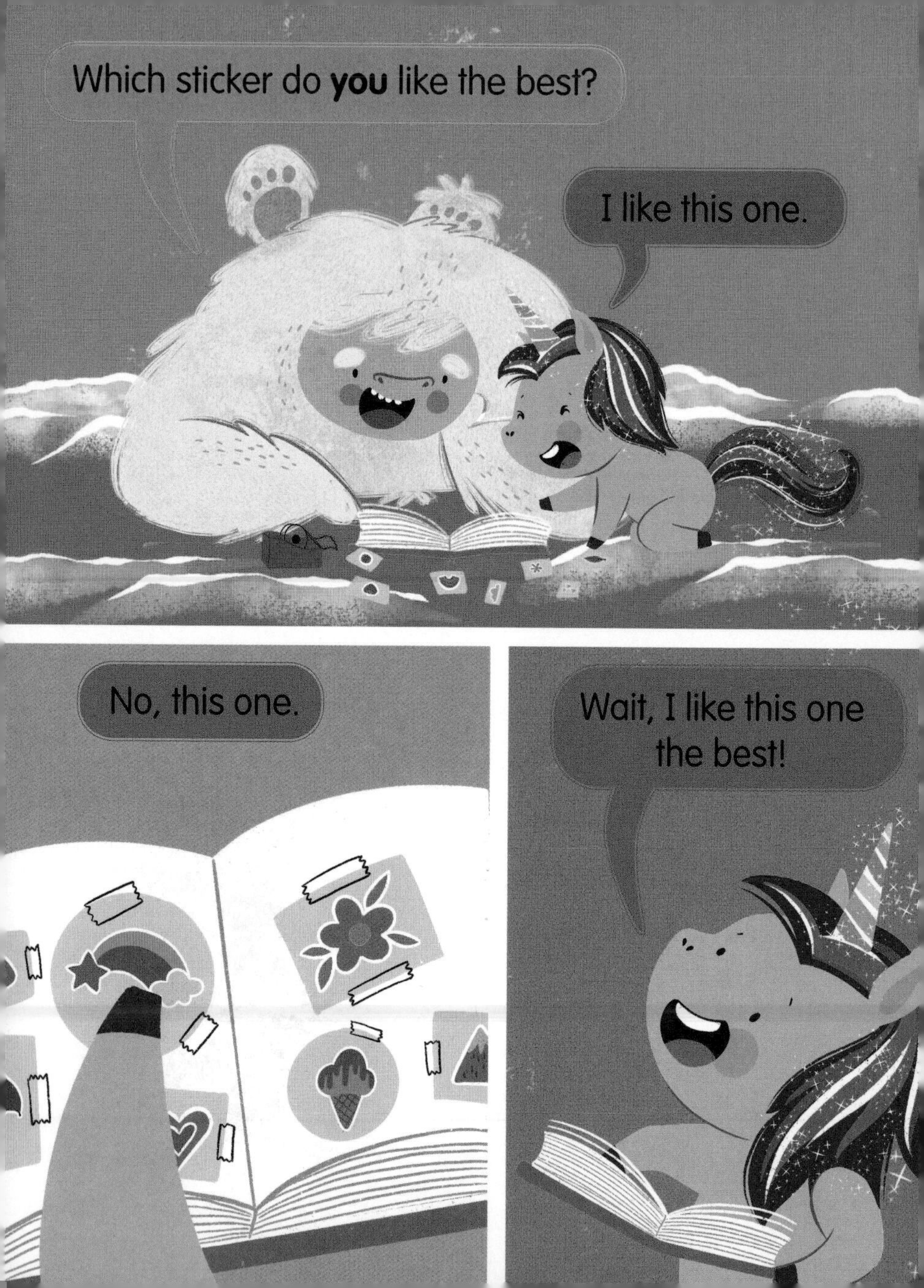
Which sticker do **you** like the best?
I like this one.
No, this one.
Wait, I like this one the best!

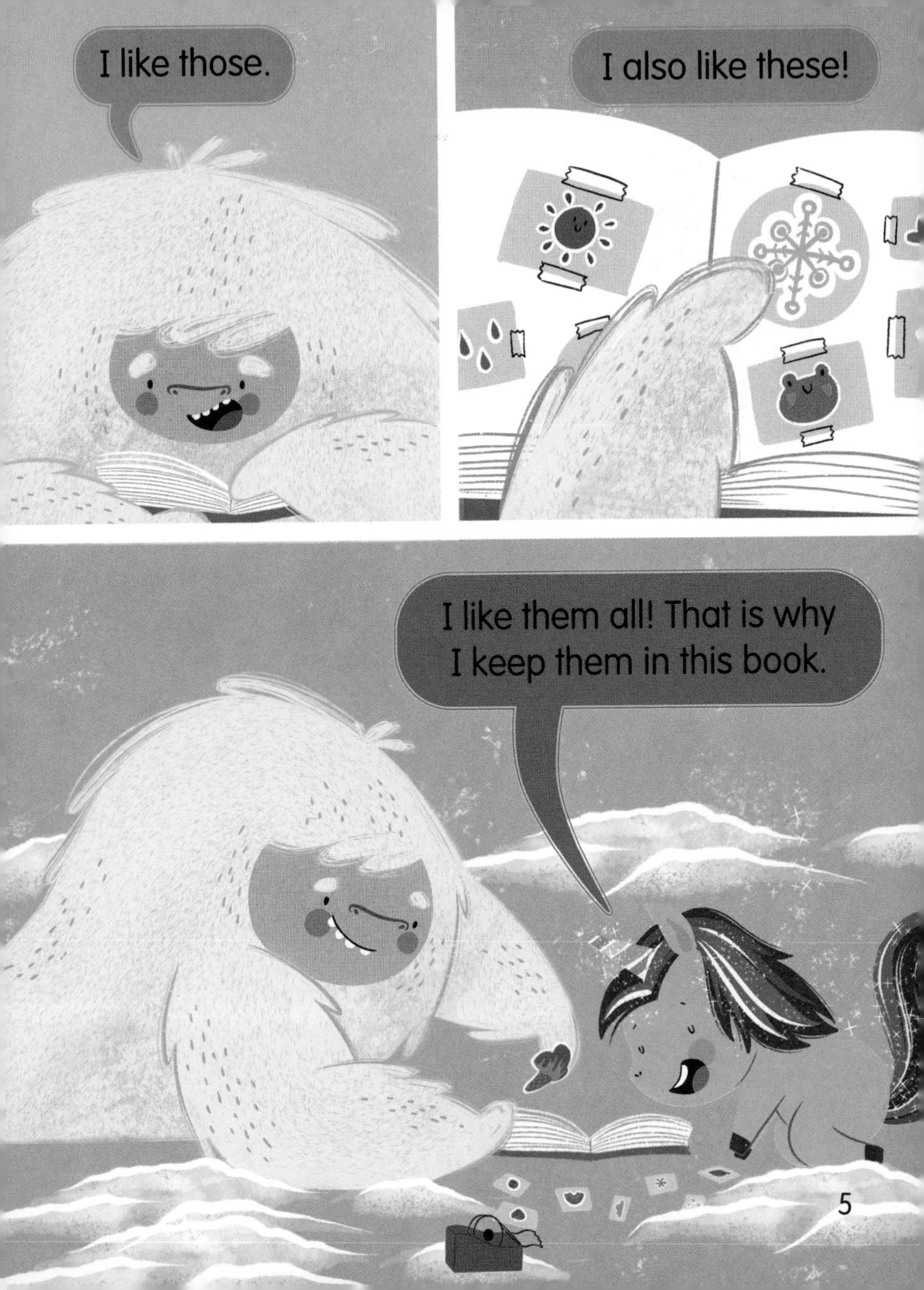
I like those.
I also like these!
I like them all! That is why I keep them in this book.

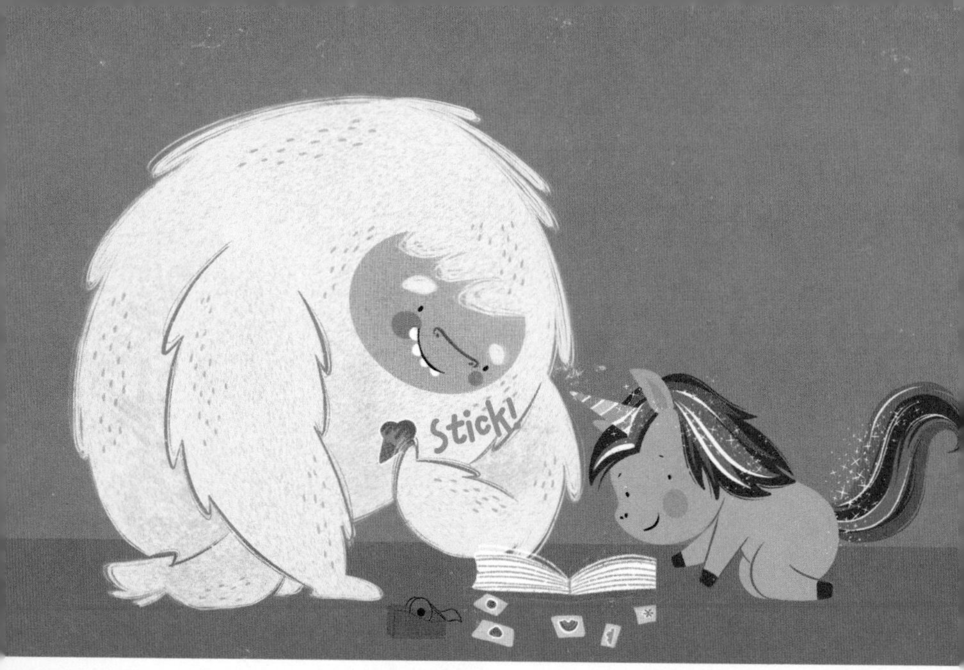
Stick!

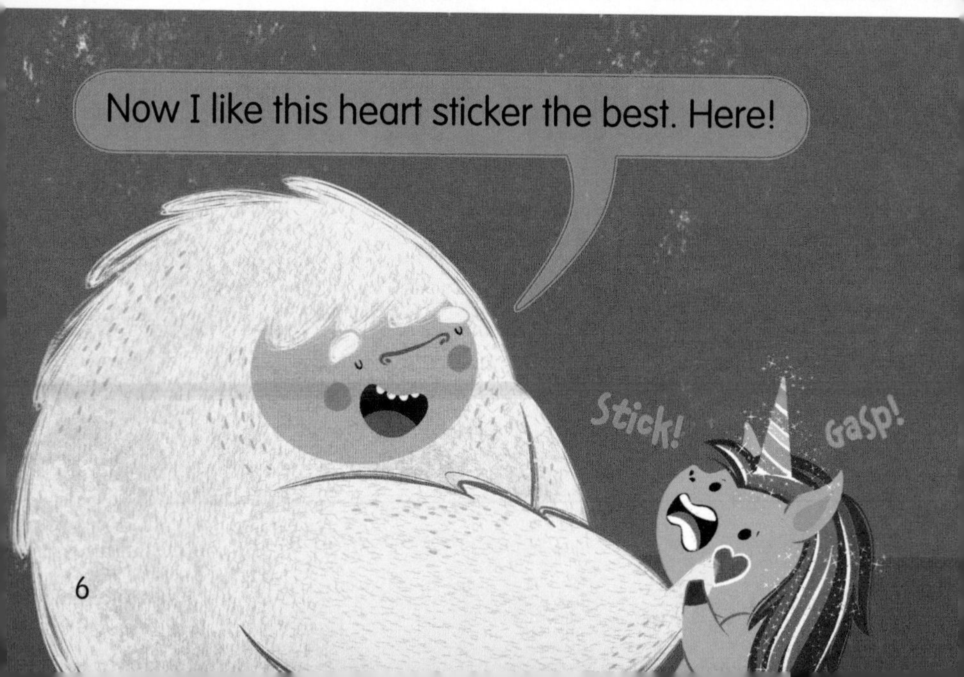
Now I like this heart sticker the best. Here!
Stick!
Gasp!

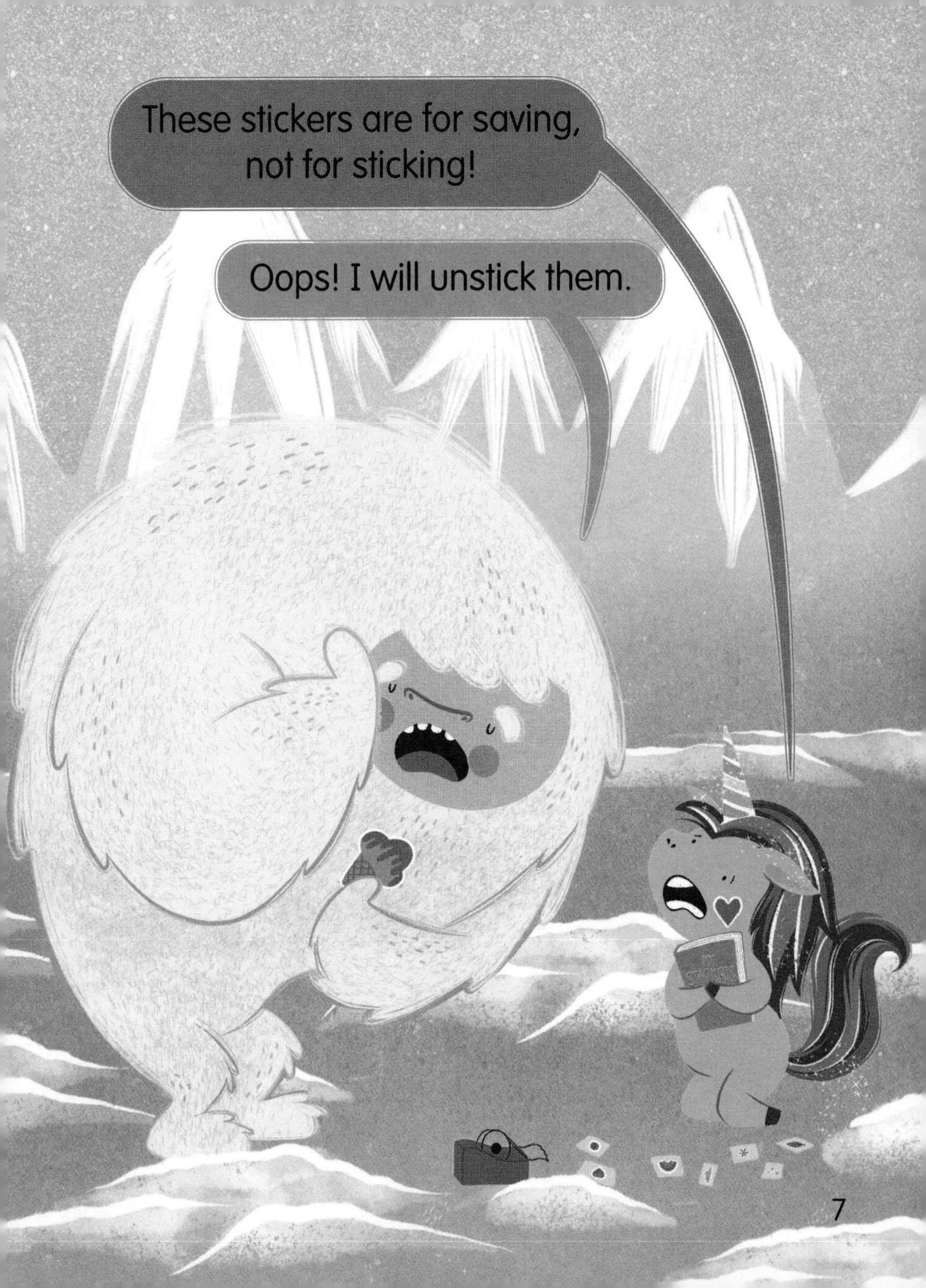
These stickers are for saving, not for sticking!
Oops! I will unstick them.

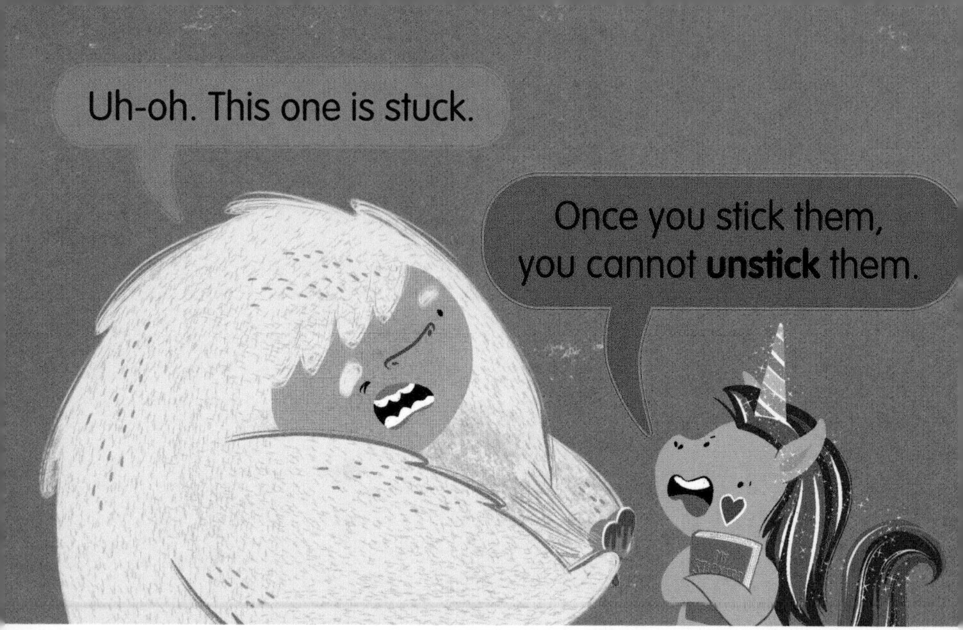
Uh-oh. This one is stuck.
Once you stick them, you cannot **unstick** them.

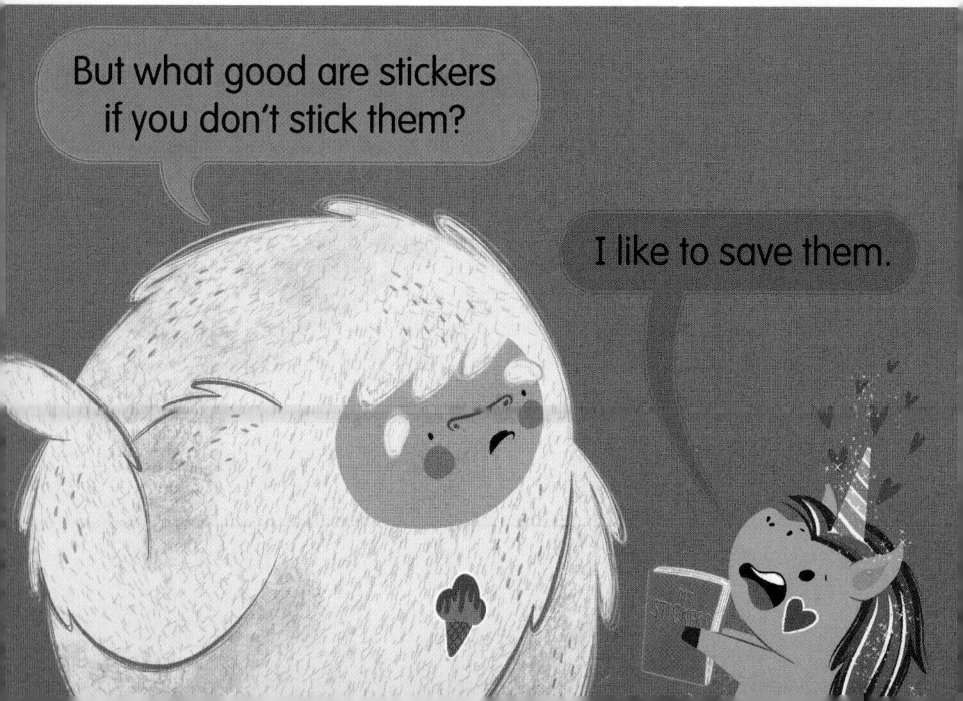
But what good are stickers if you don't stick them?
I like to save them.

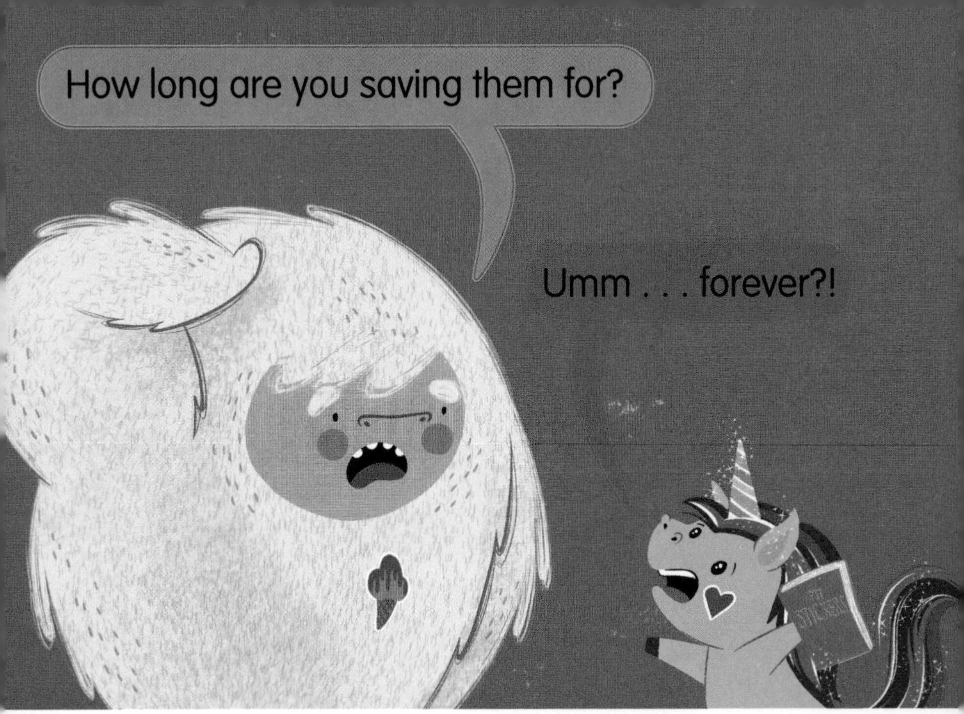
How long are you saving them for?
Umm . . . forever?!

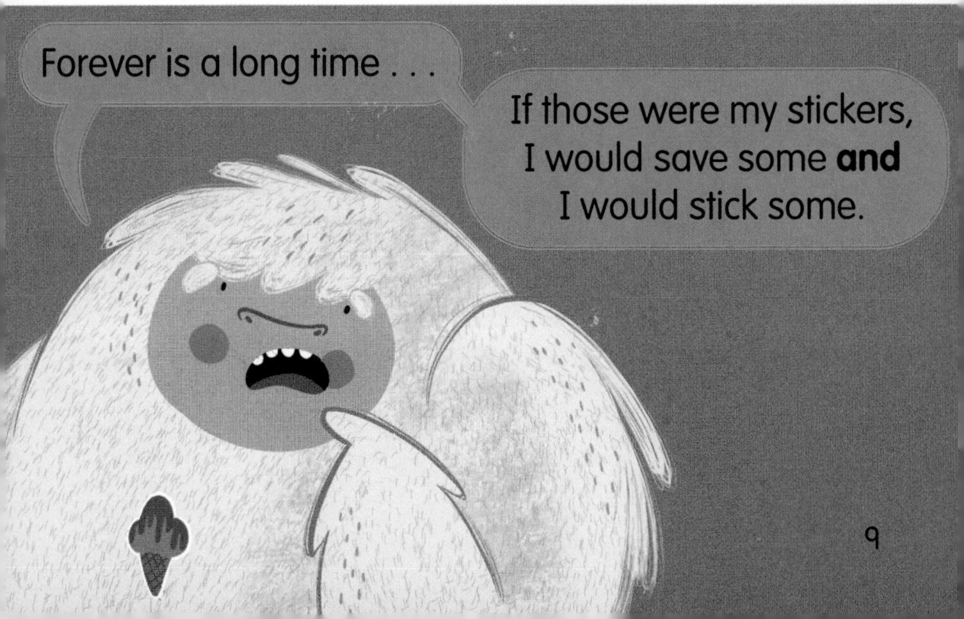
Forever is a long time . . .
If those were my stickers, I would save some **and** I would stick some.

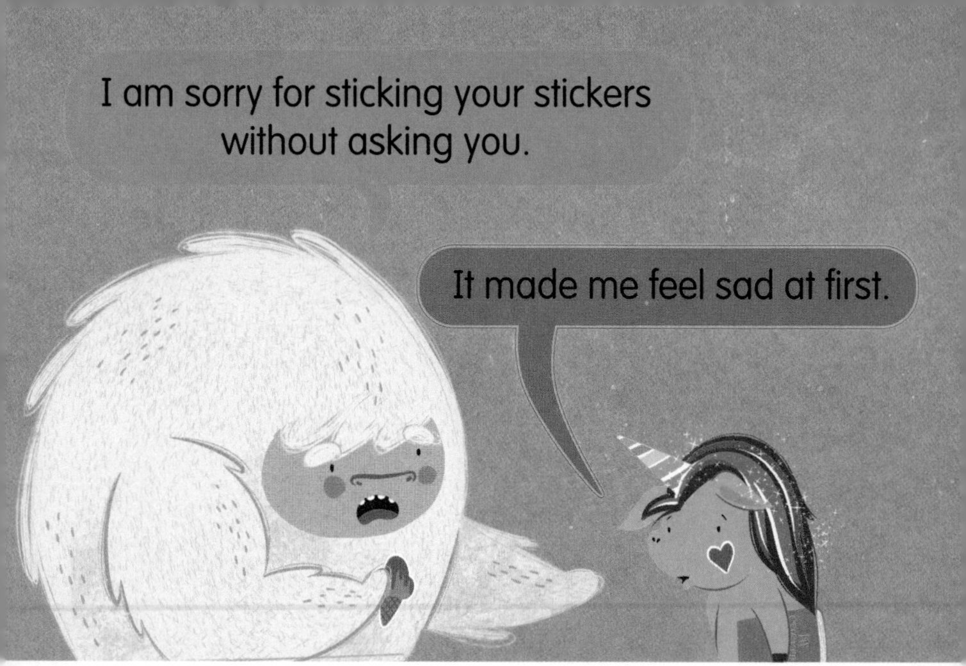
I am sorry for sticking your stickers without asking you.
It made me feel sad at first.

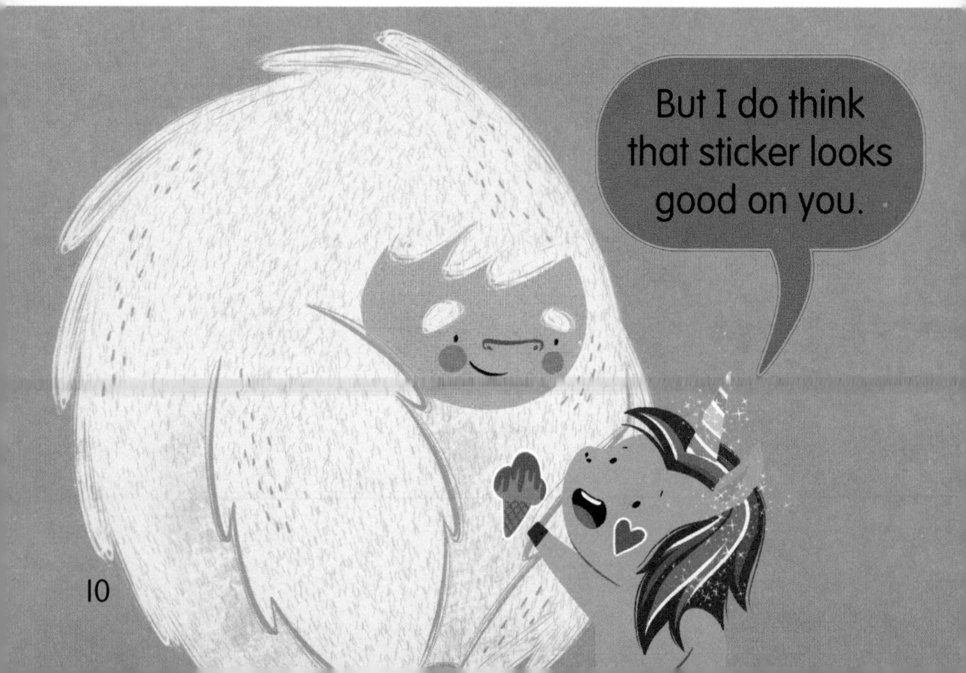
But I do think that sticker looks good on you.

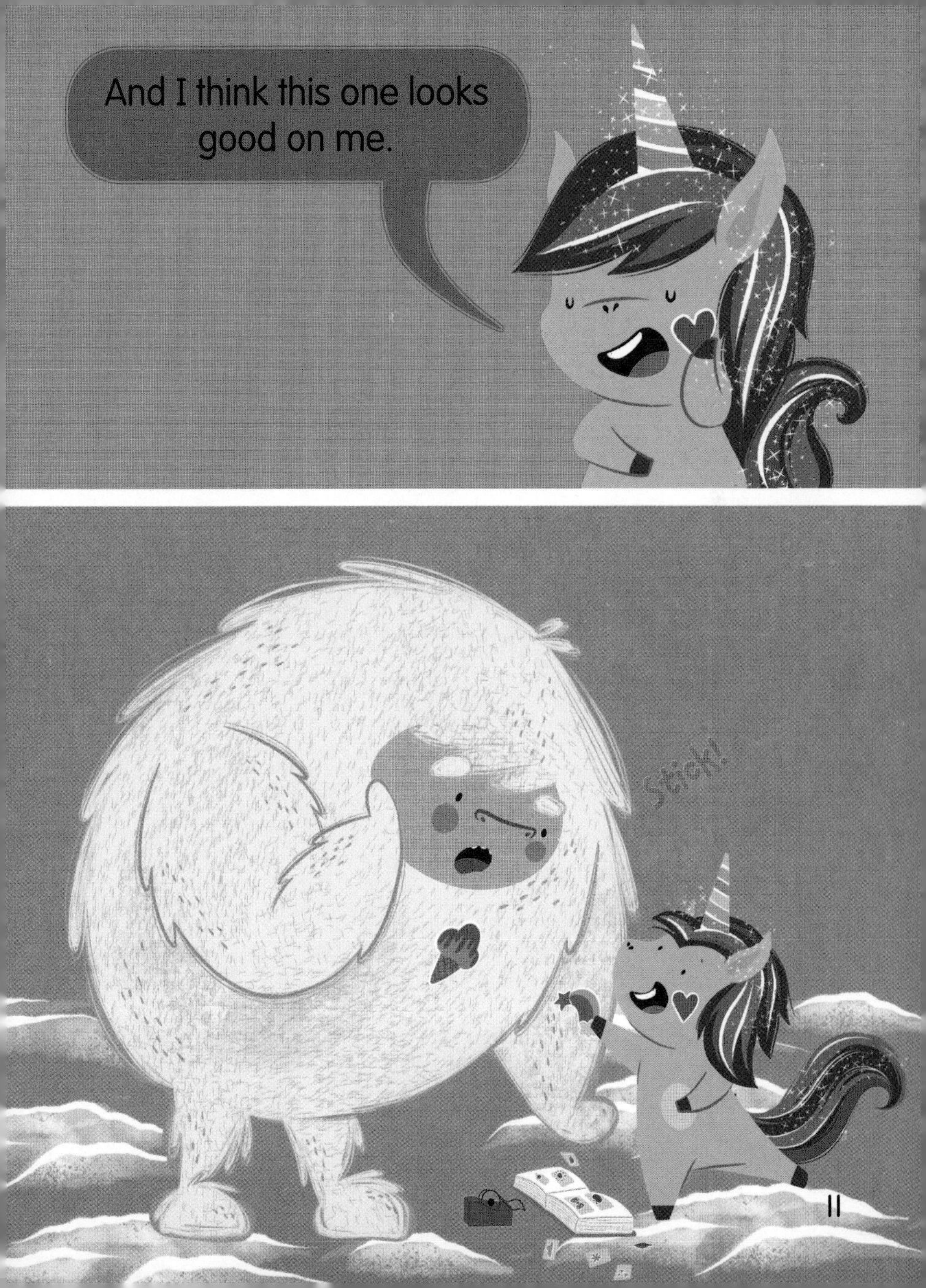
And I think this one looks good on me.
Stick!

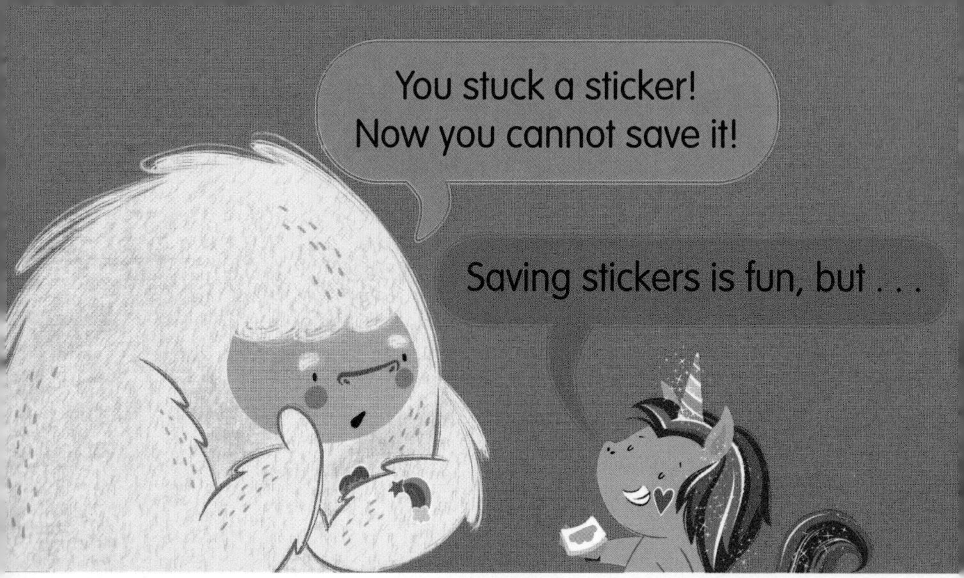

You stuck a sticker!
Now you cannot save it!
Saving stickers is fun, but . . .

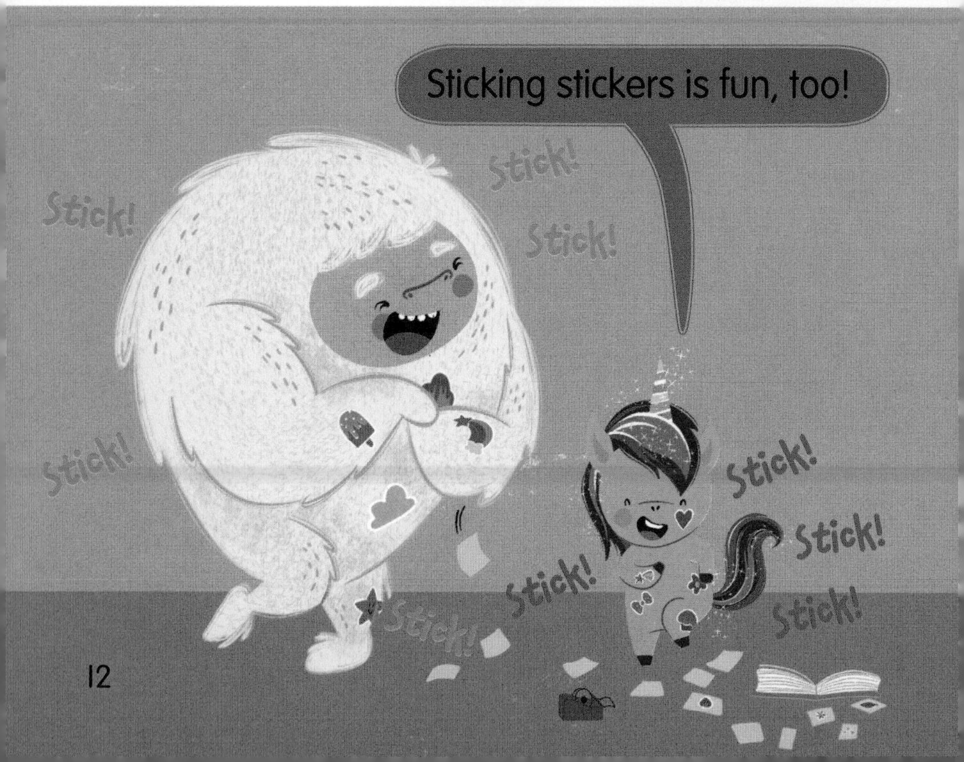

Sticking stickers is fun, too!
Stick!
Stick!
Stick!
Stick!
Stick!
Stick!
Stick!
Stick!
Stick!

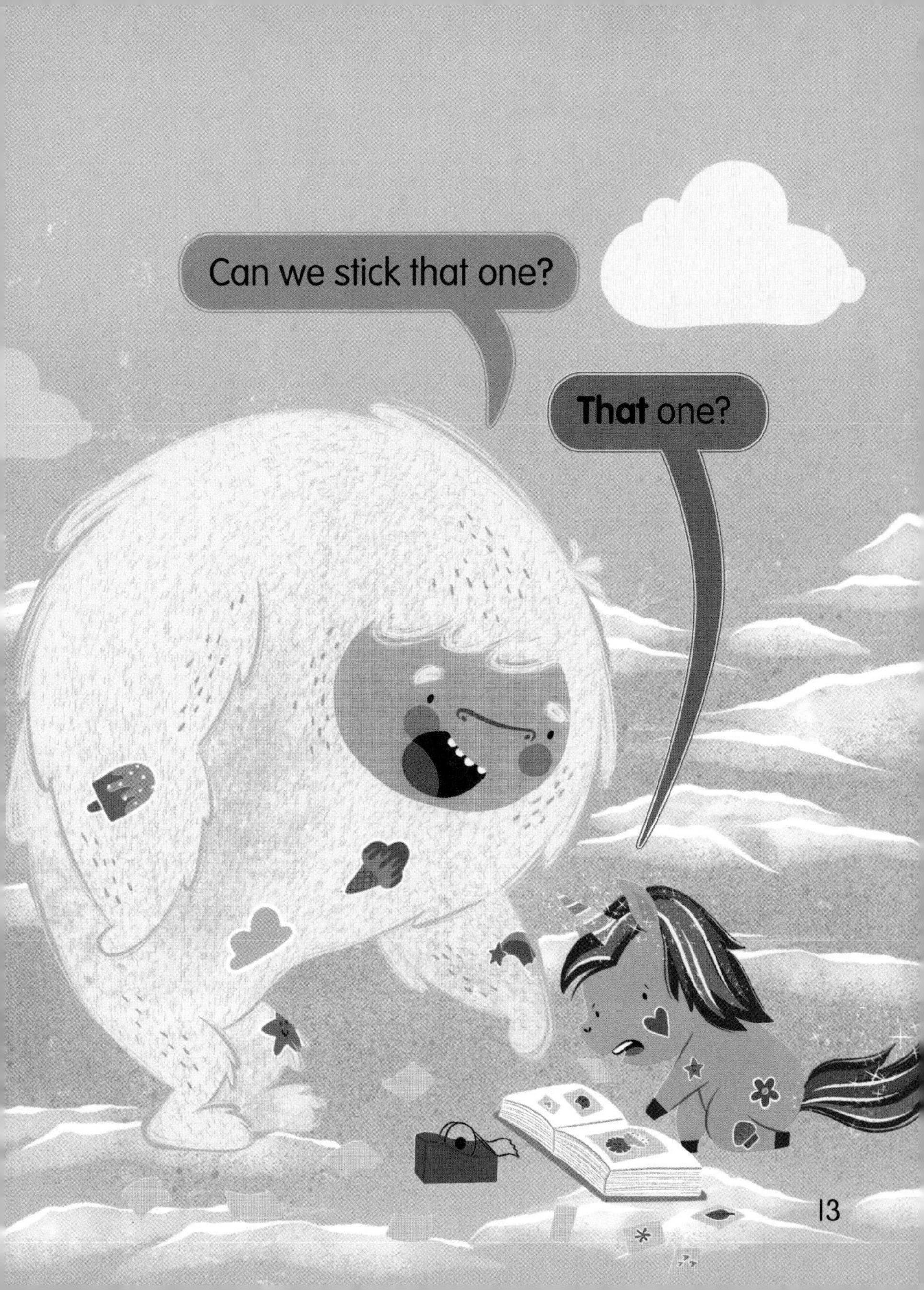

Can we stick that one?
That one?

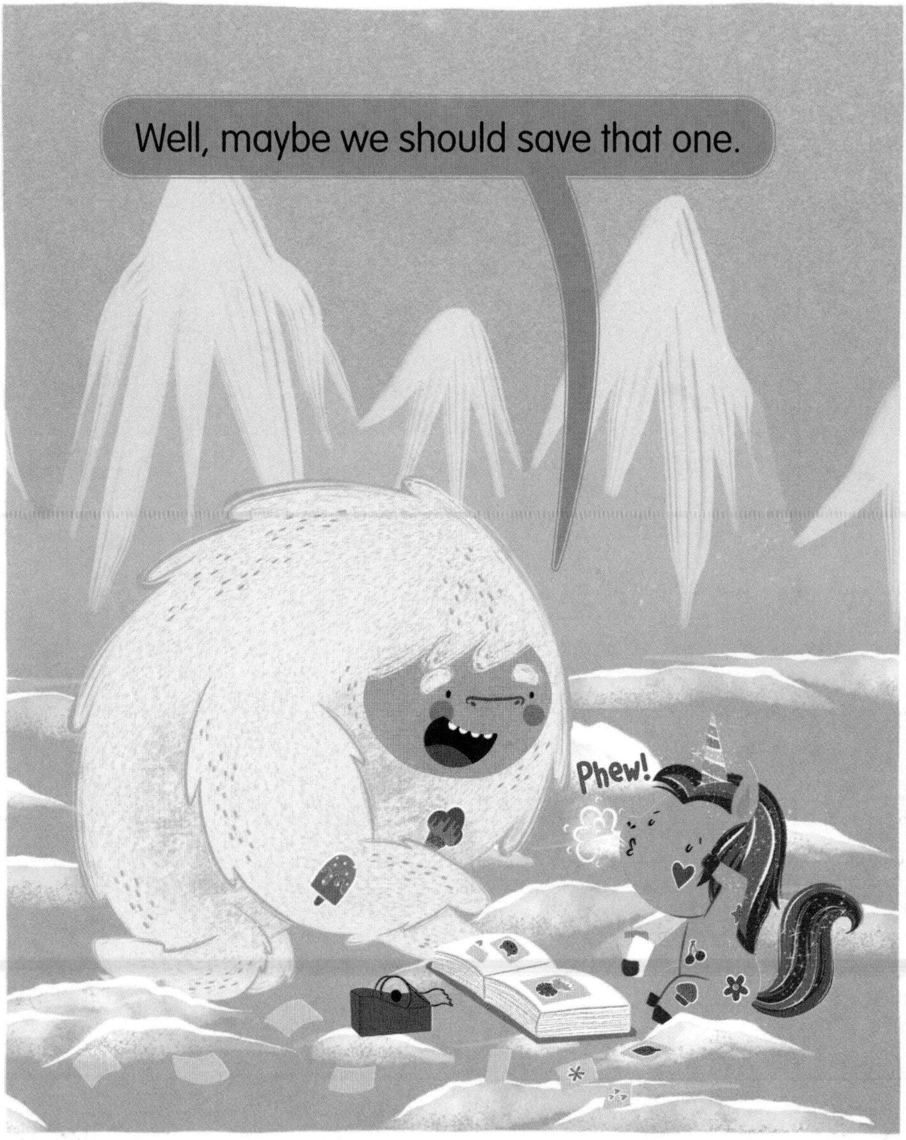
Well, maybe we should save that one.
Phew!

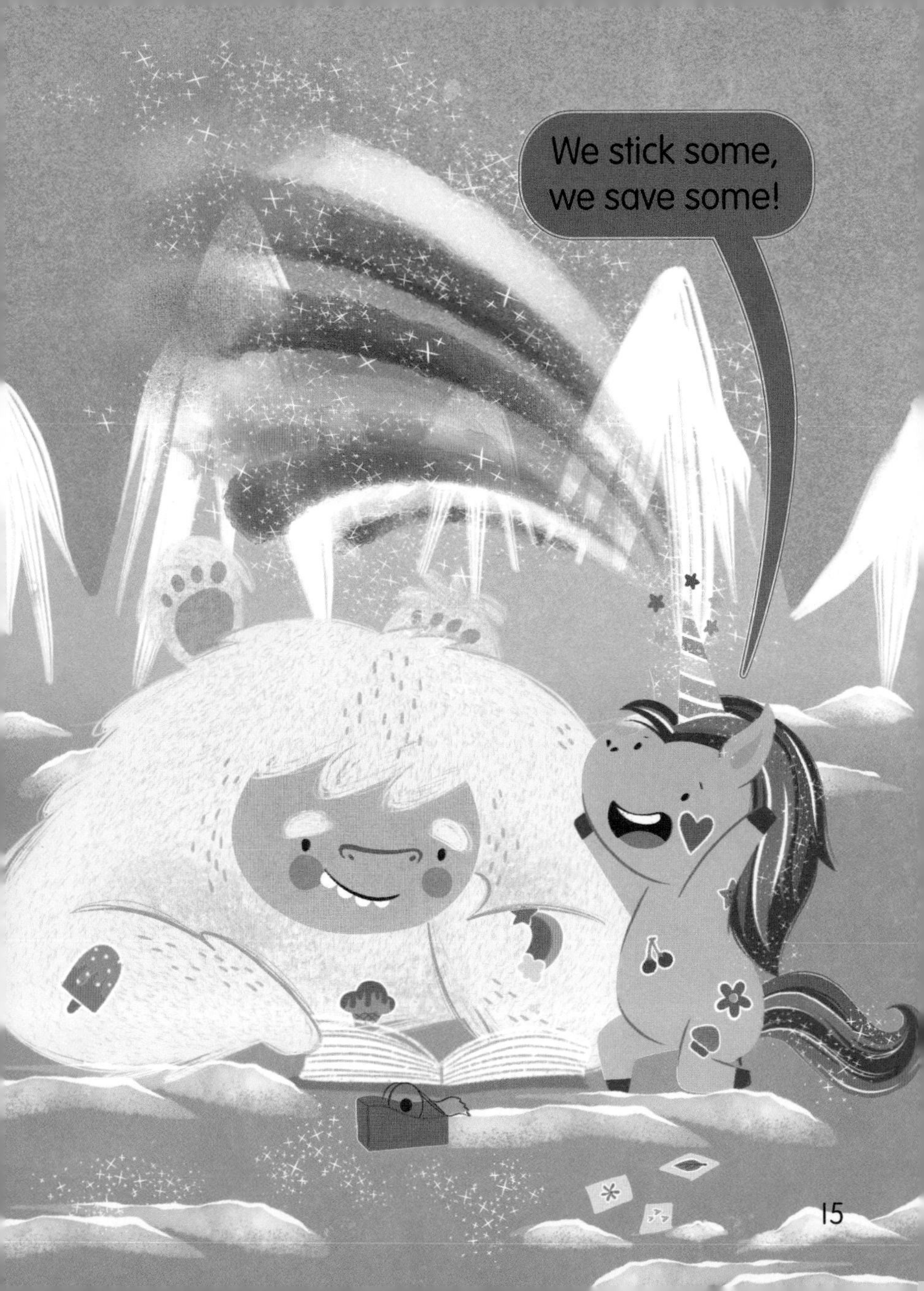
We stick some,
we save some!

Let's Roll

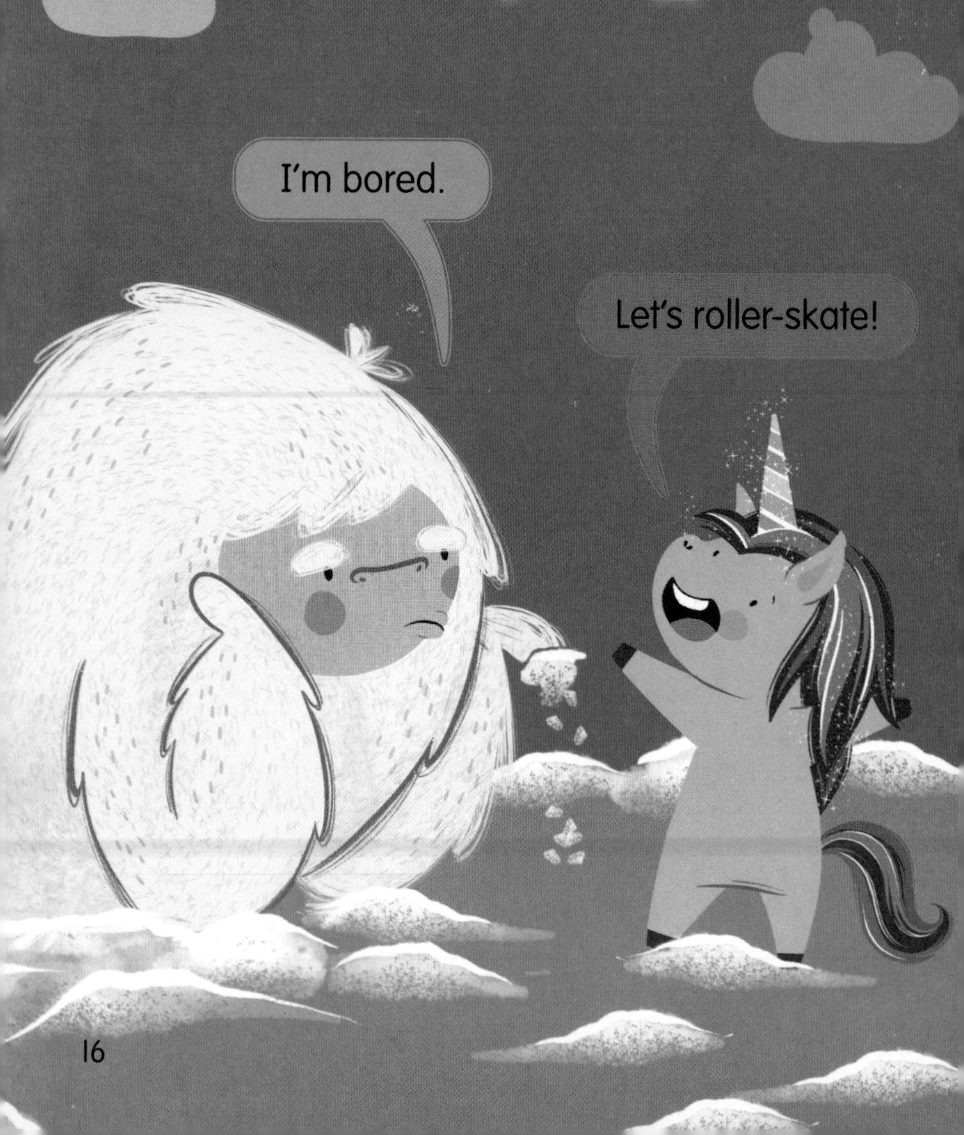

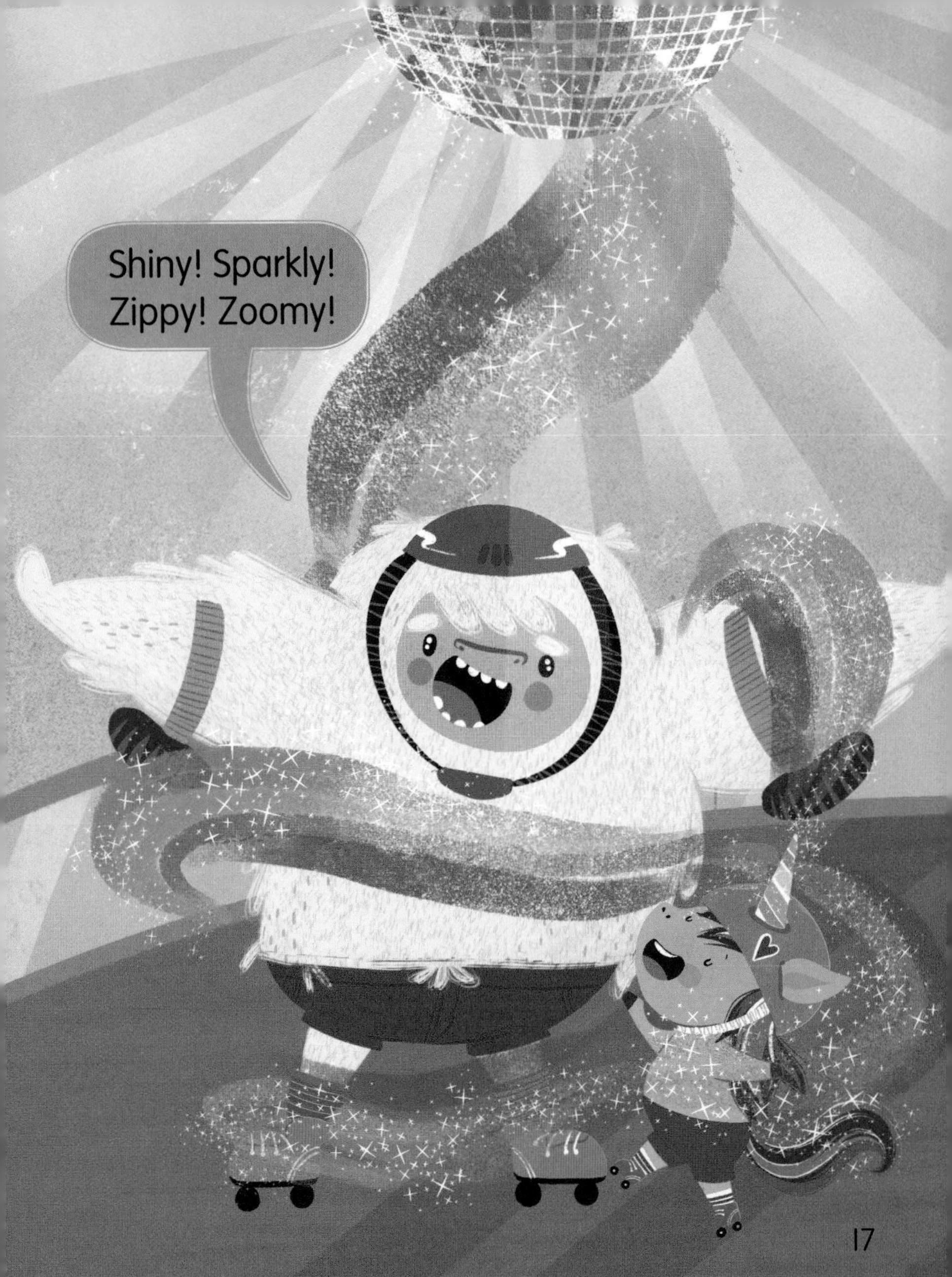
Shiny! Sparkly!
Zippy! Zoomy!

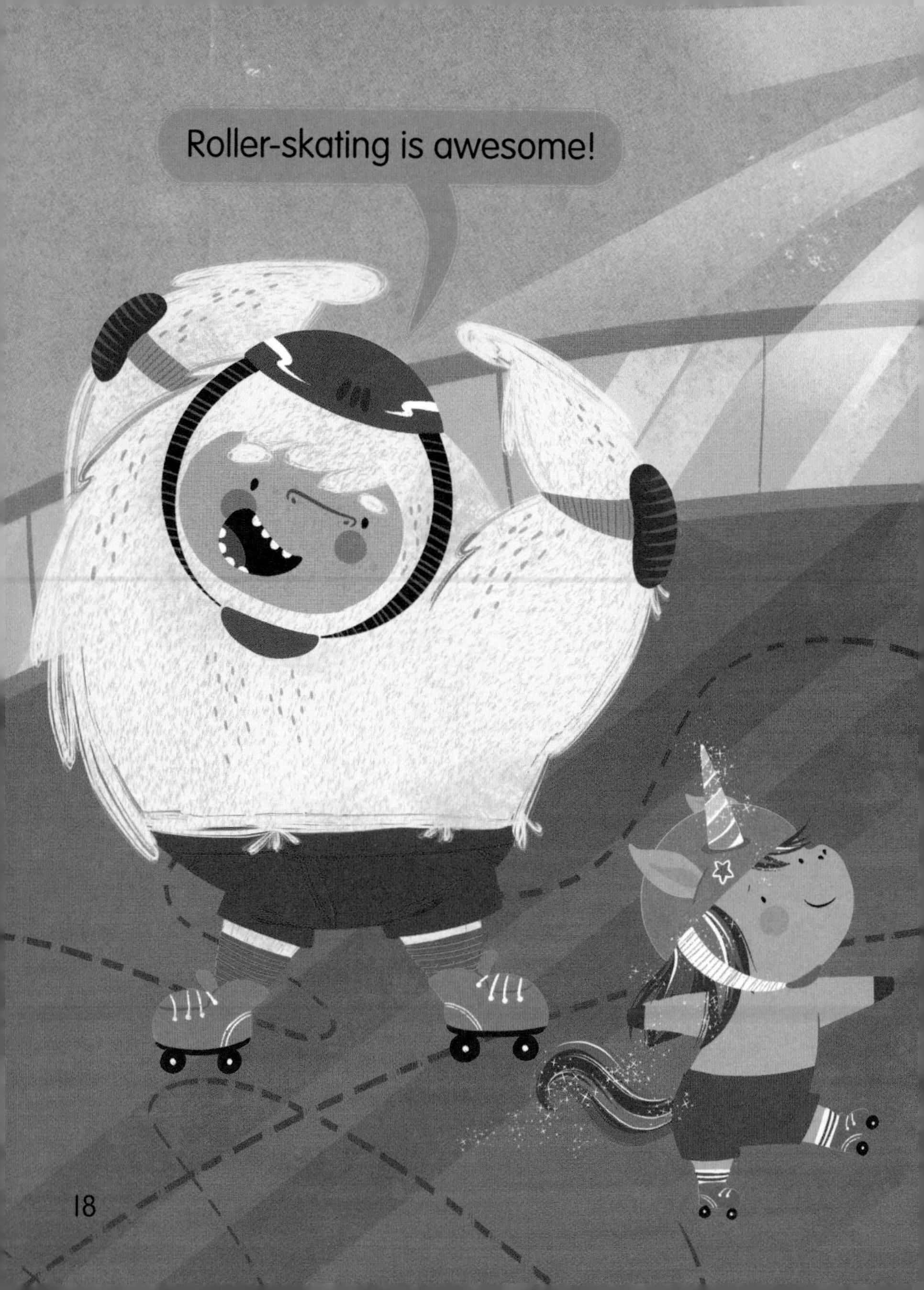
Roller-skating is awesome!

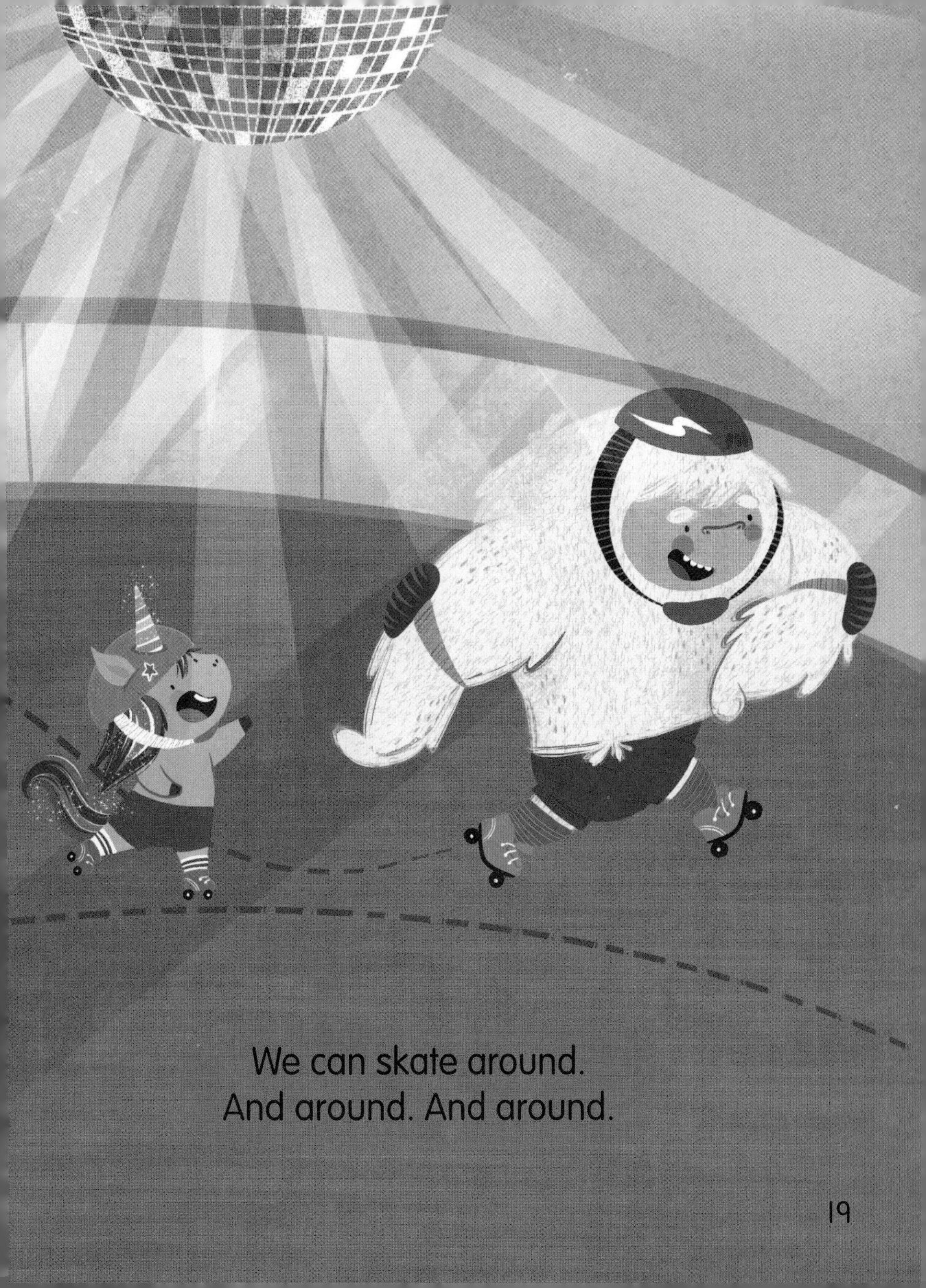

We can skate around.
And around. And around.

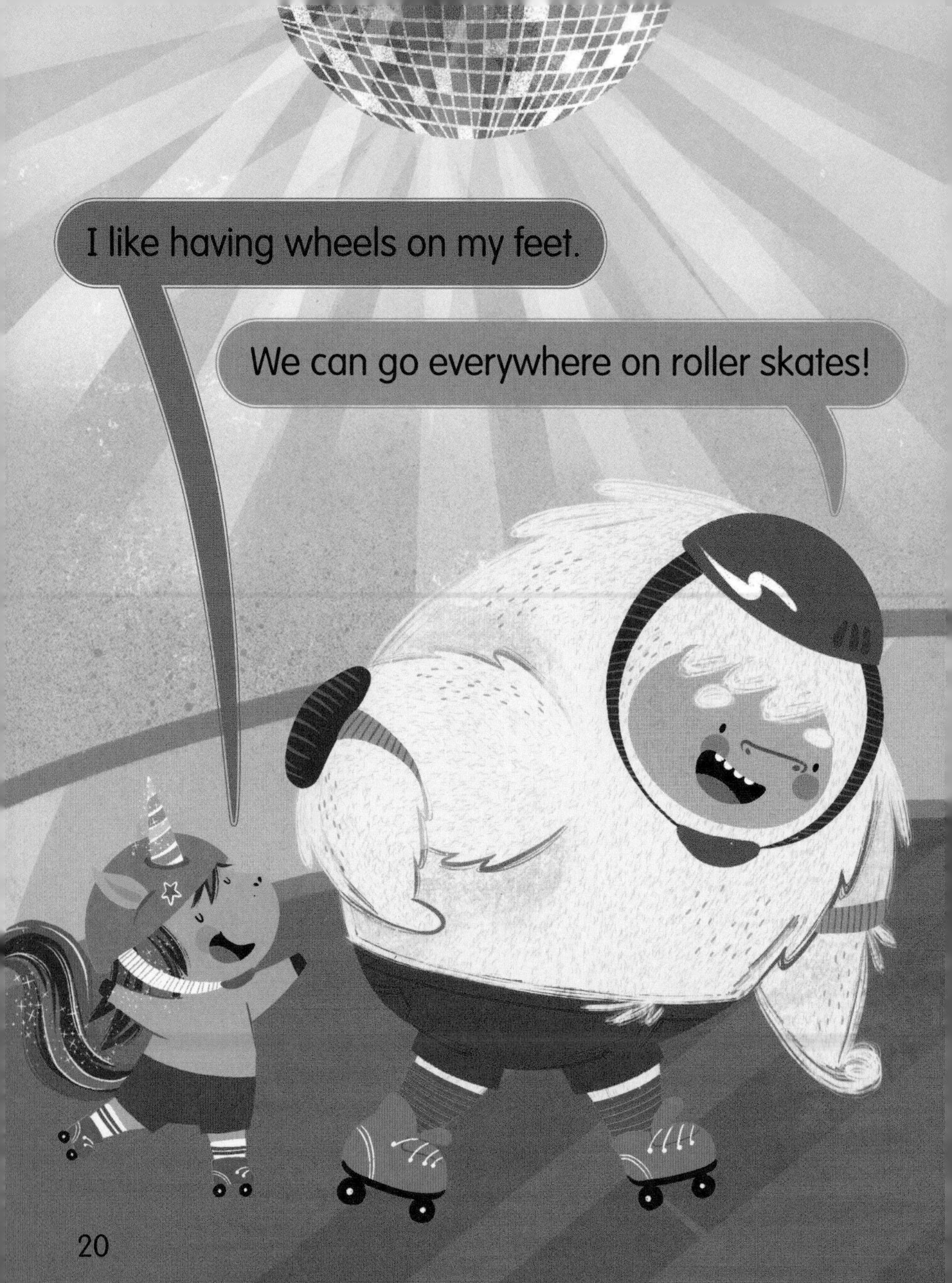
I like having wheels on my feet.
We can go everywhere on roller skates!

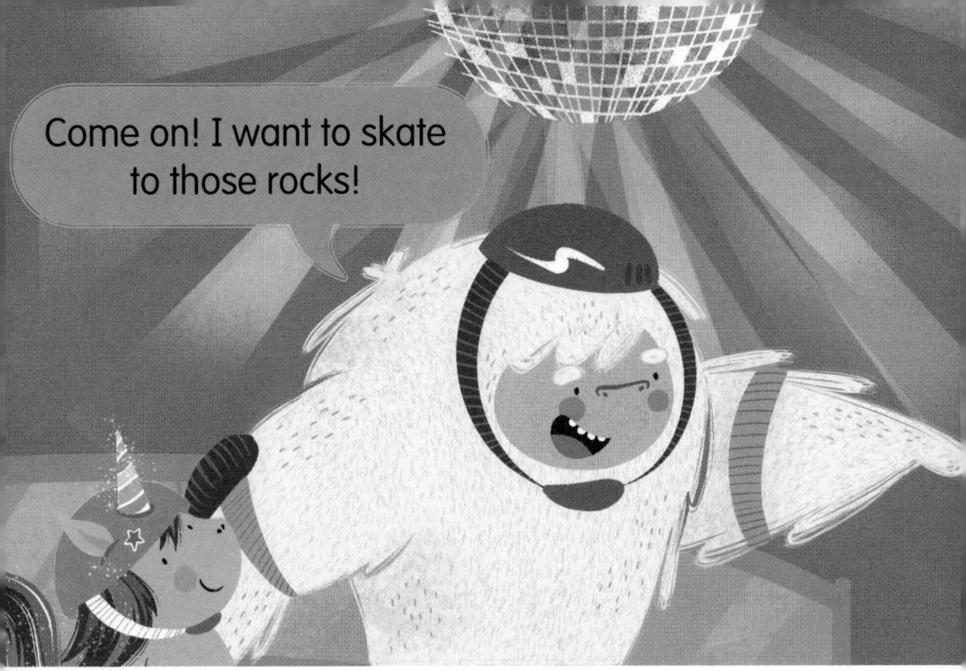
Come on! I want to skate to those rocks!

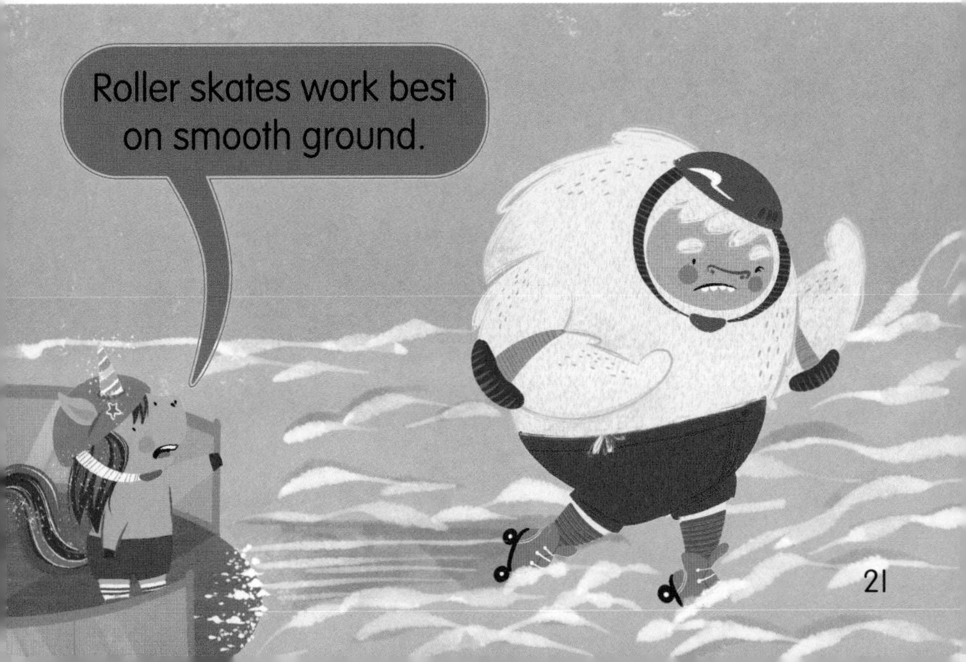
Roller skates work best on smooth ground.

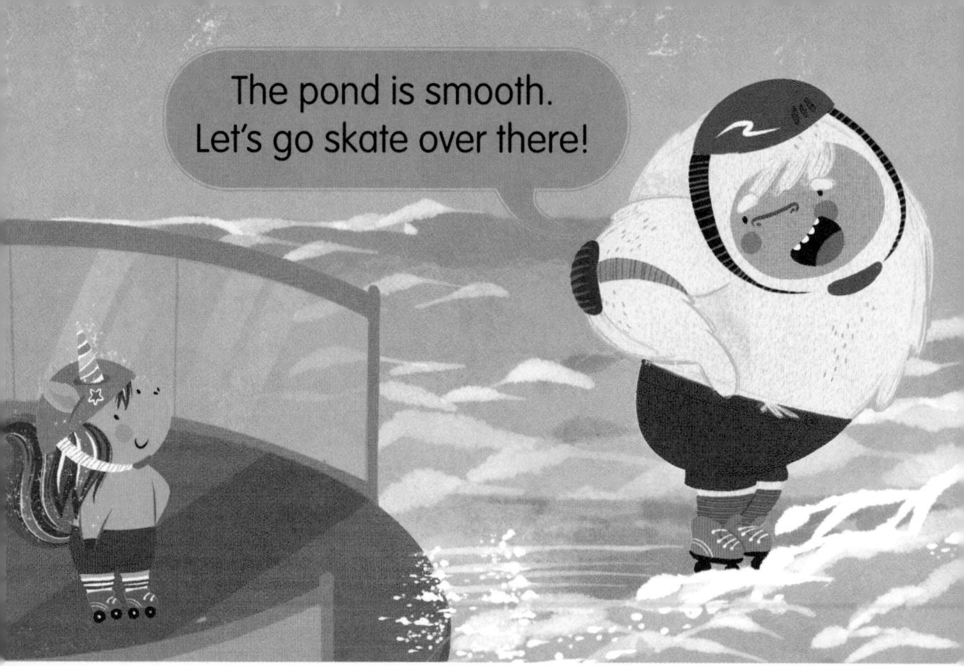
The pond is smooth. Let's go skate over there!

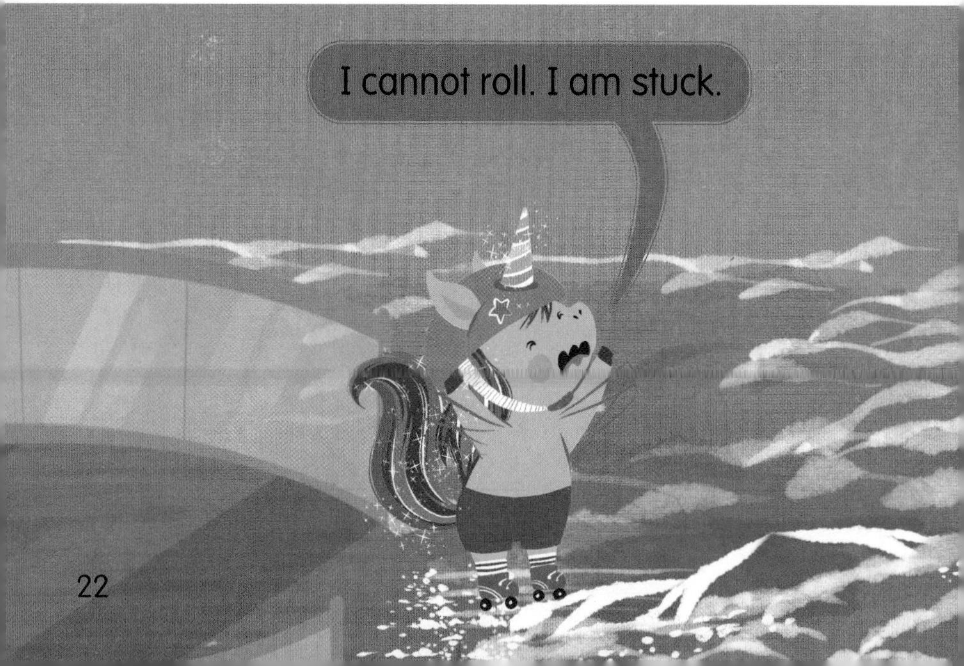
I cannot roll. I am stuck.

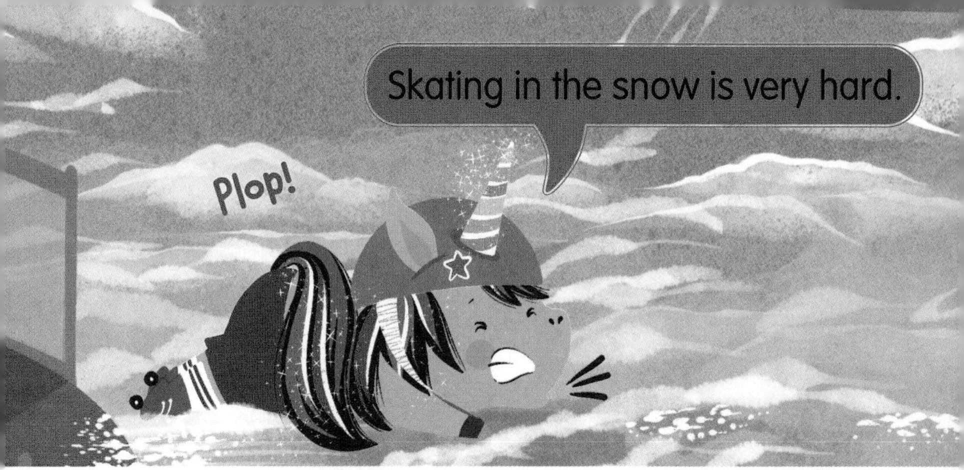
Skating in the snow is very hard.
Plop!

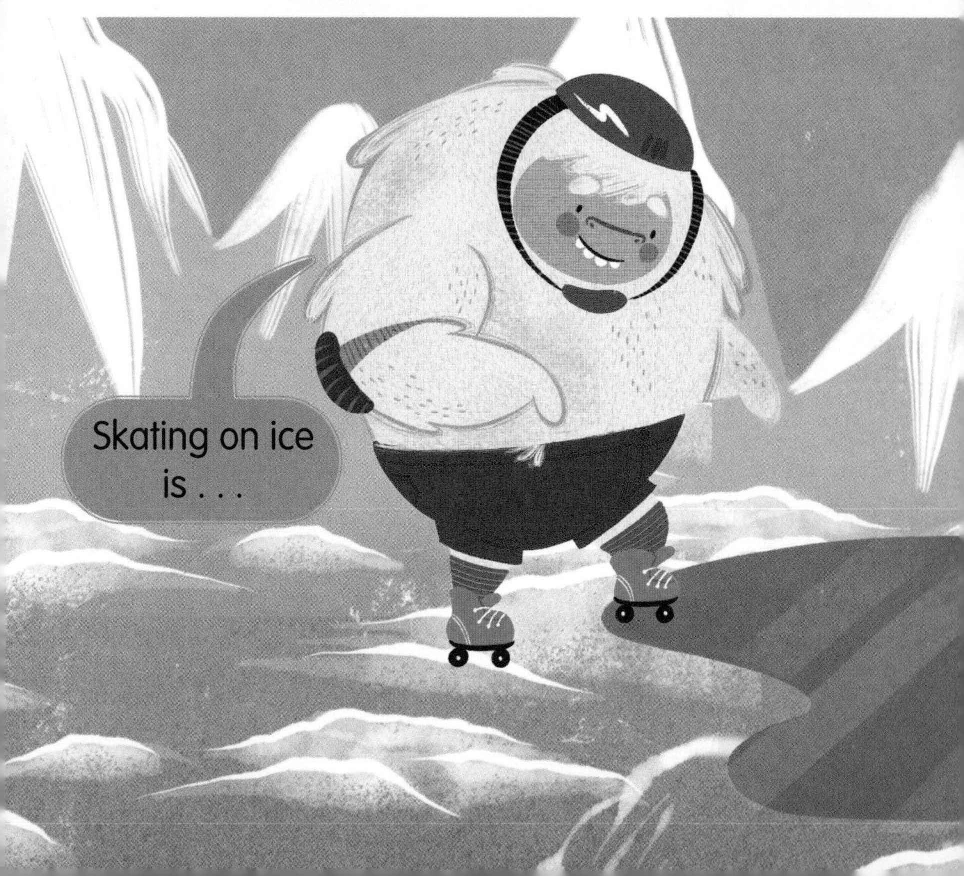
Skating on ice
is . . .

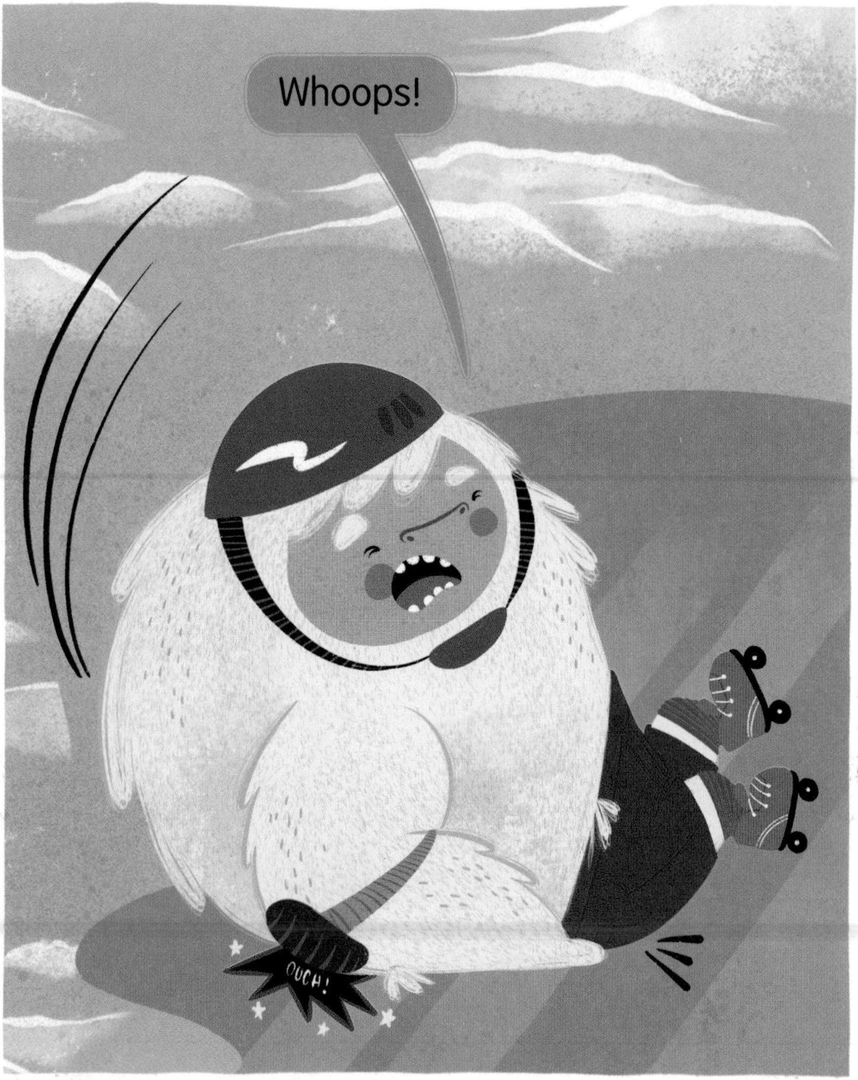
Whoops!
OUCH!

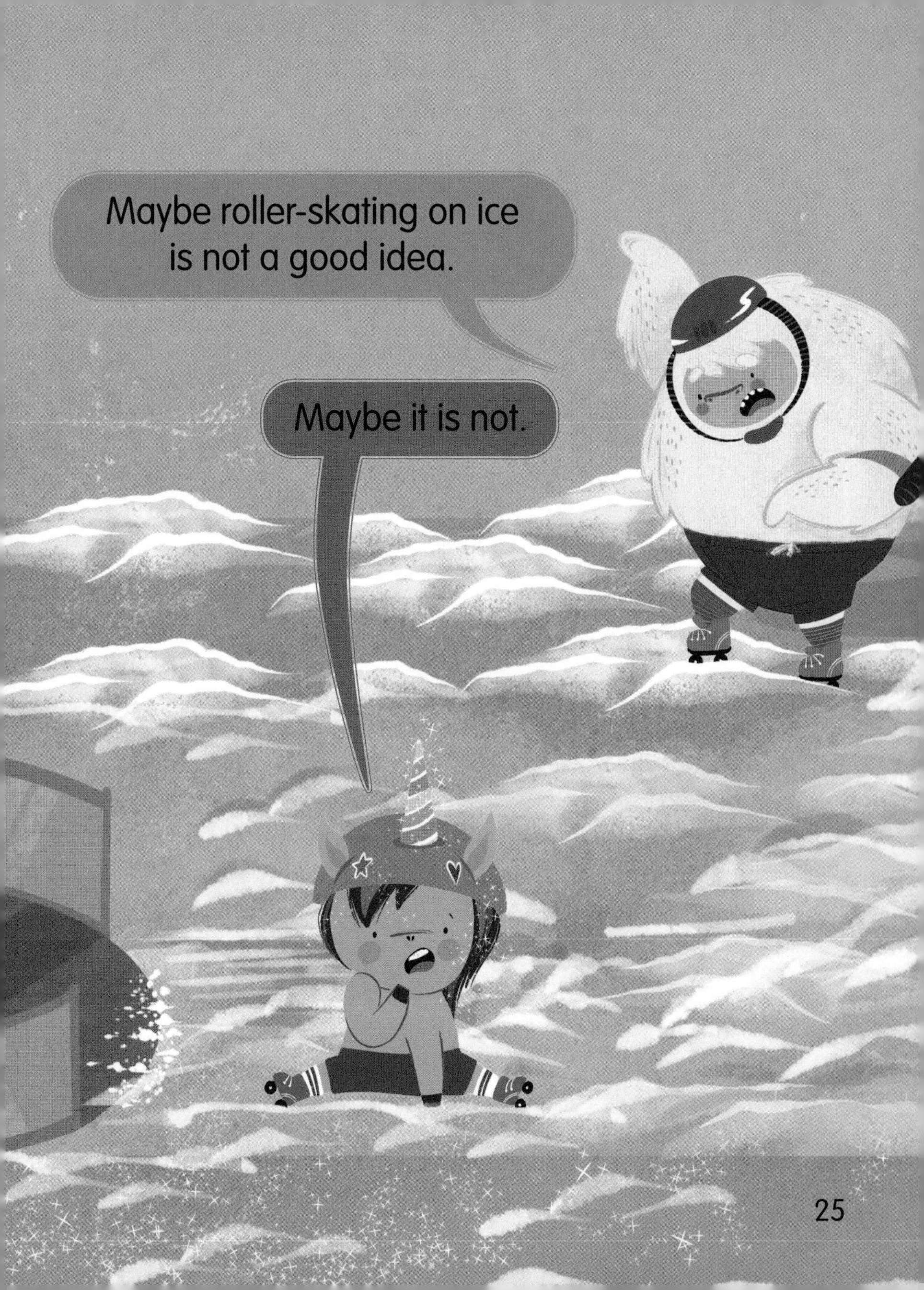

Maybe roller-skating on ice is not a good idea.
Maybe it is not.

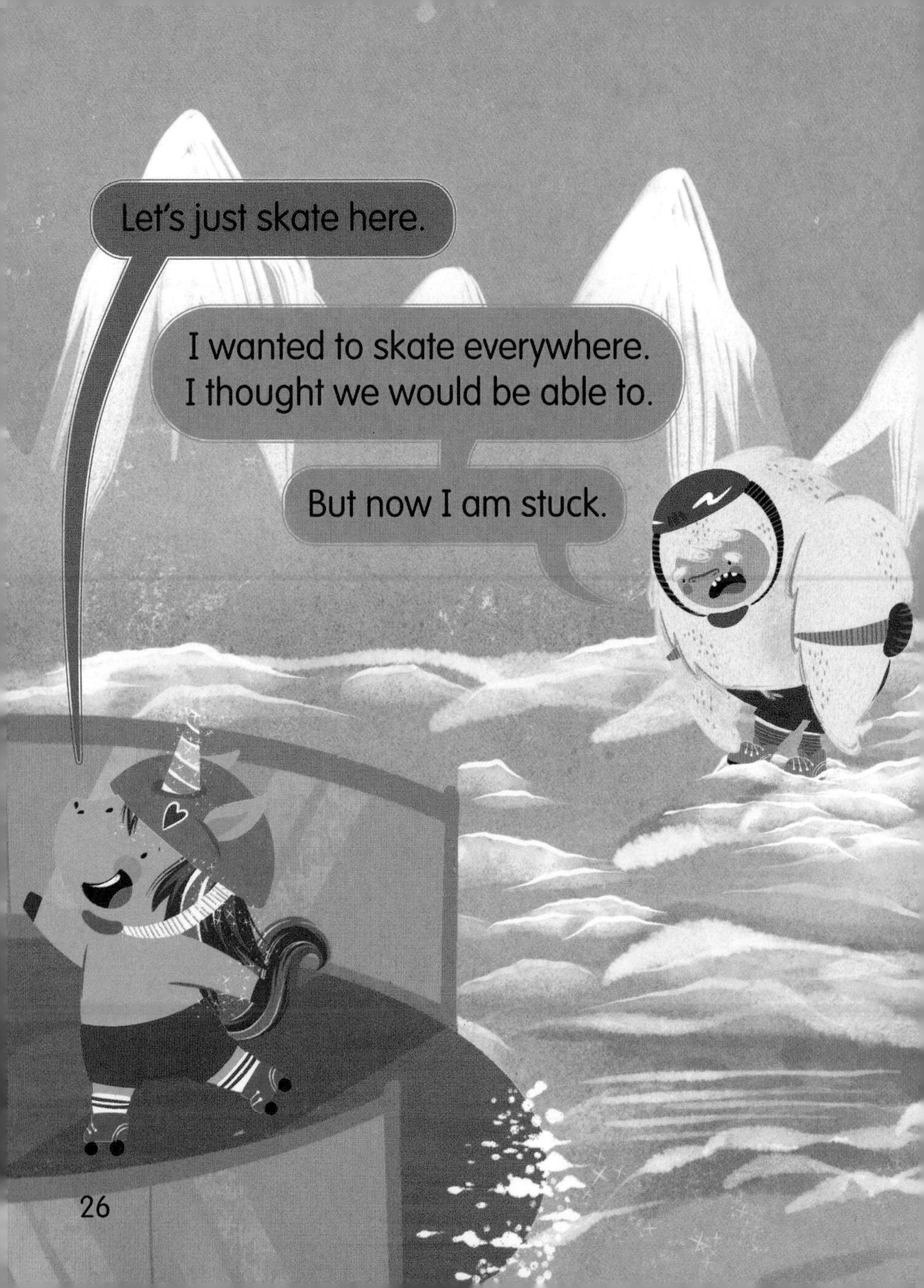
Let's just skate here.
I wanted to skate everywhere. I thought we would be able to.
But now I am stuck.

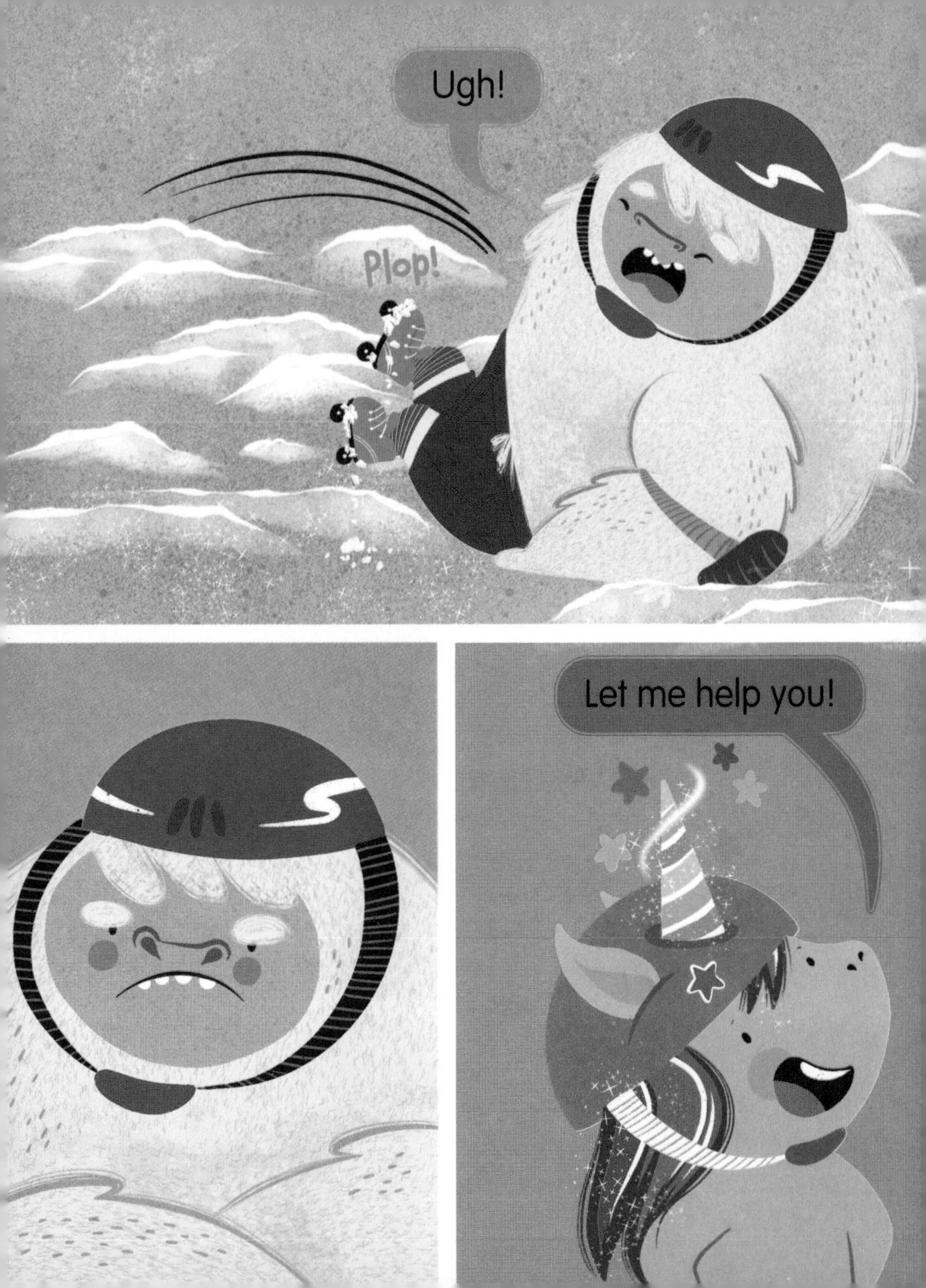
Ugh!
Plop!
Let me help you!

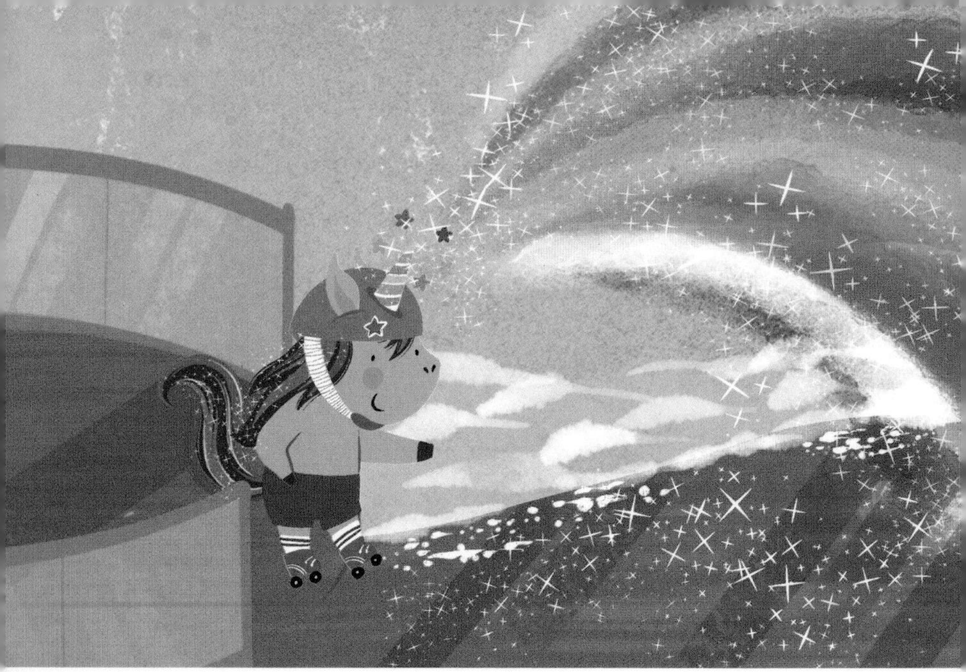

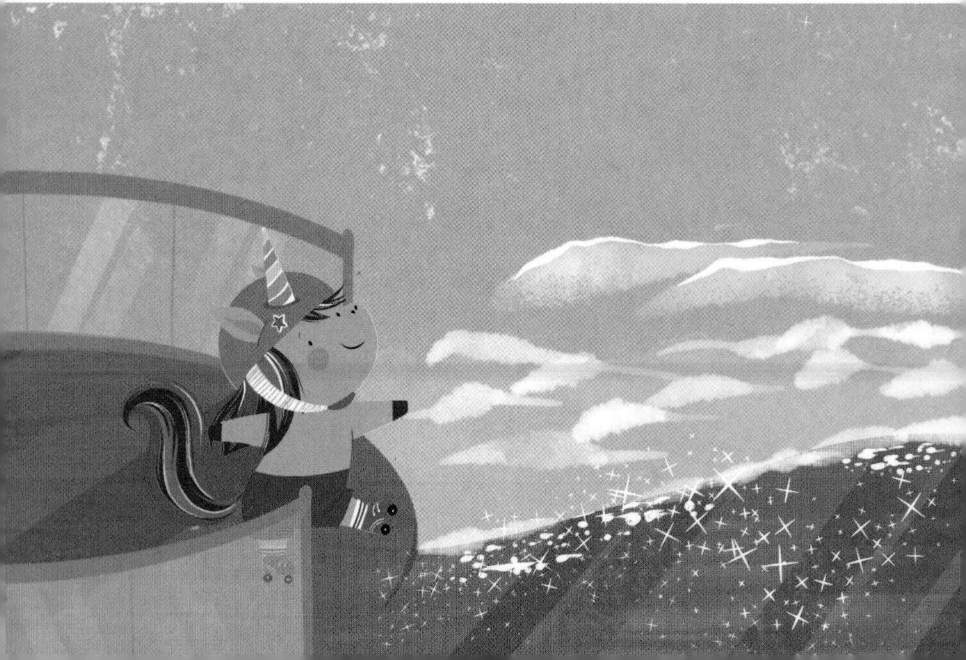

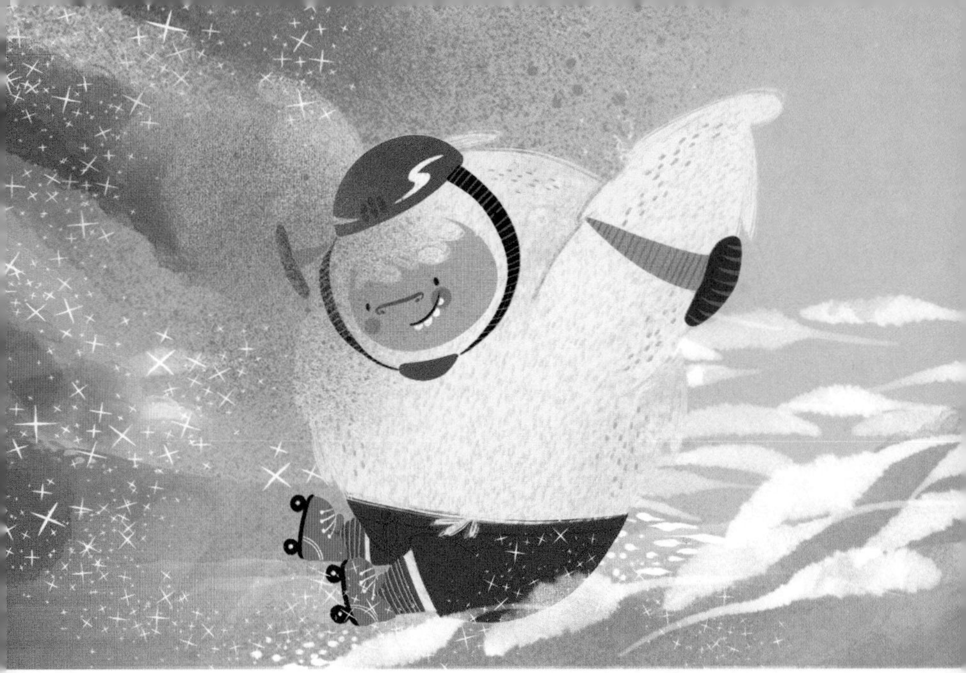

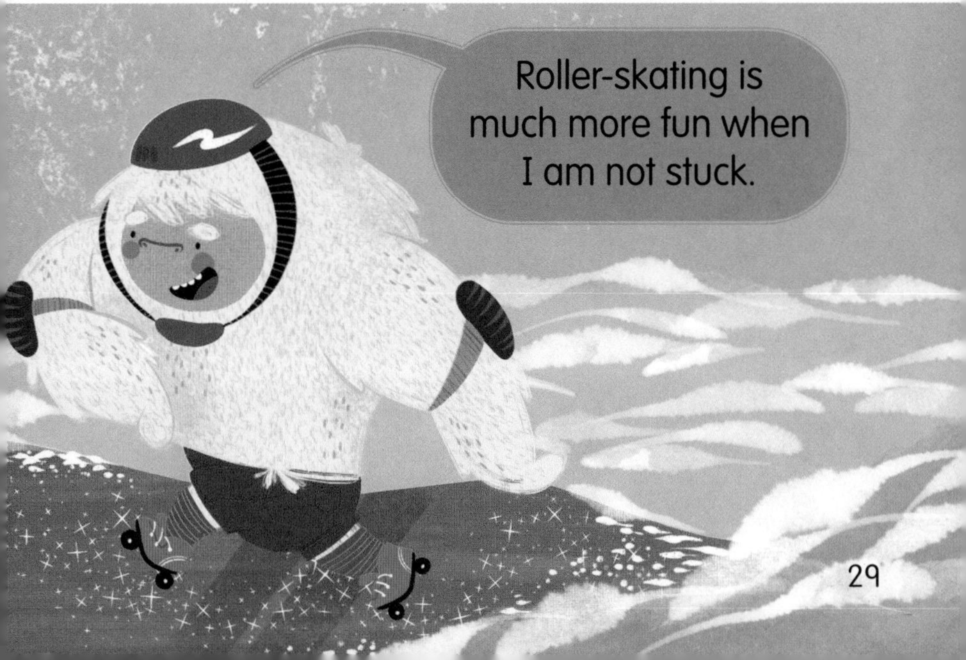
Roller-skating is much more fun when I am not stuck.

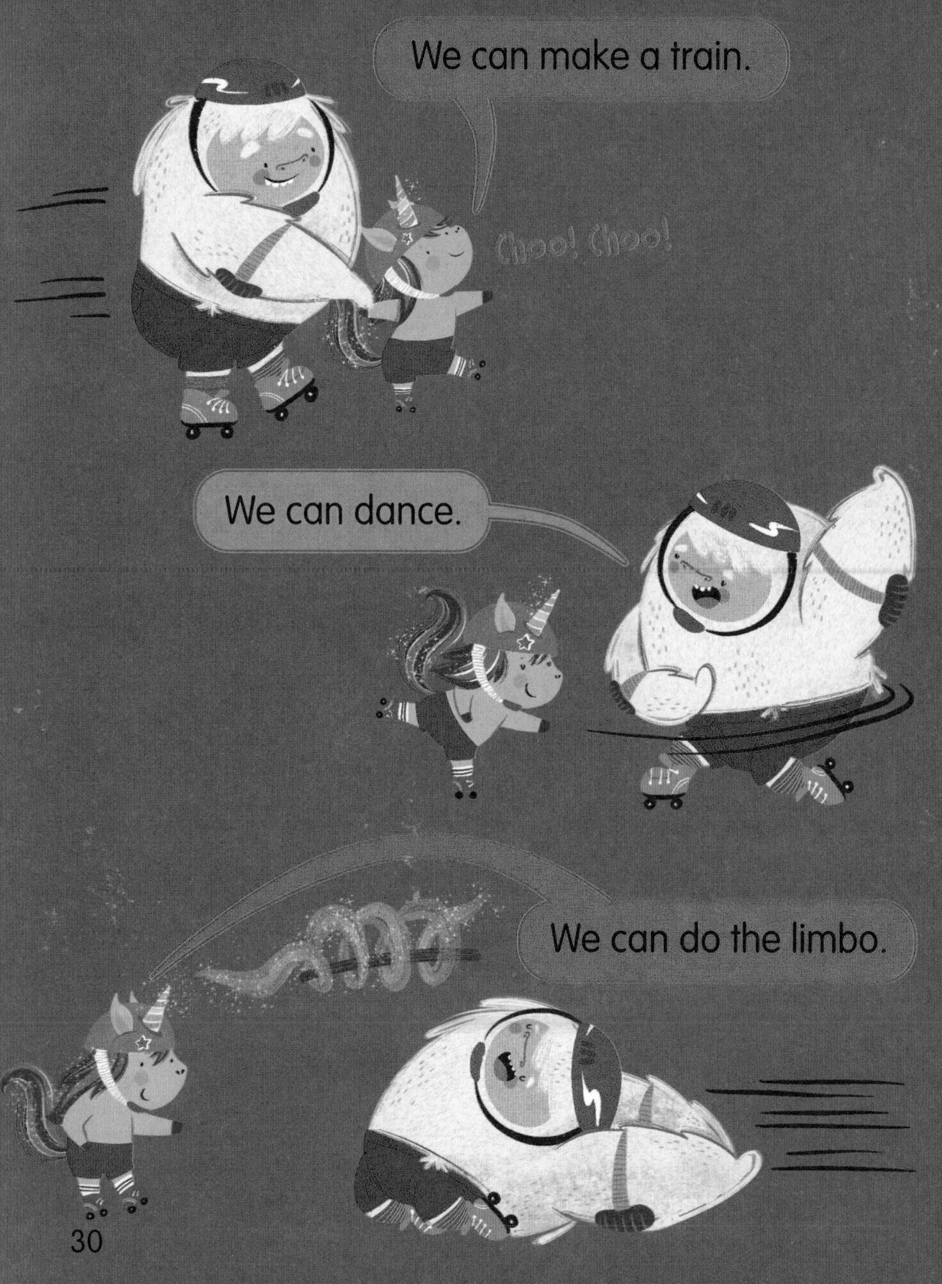
We can make a train.
Choo! Choo!
We can dance.
We can do the limbo.

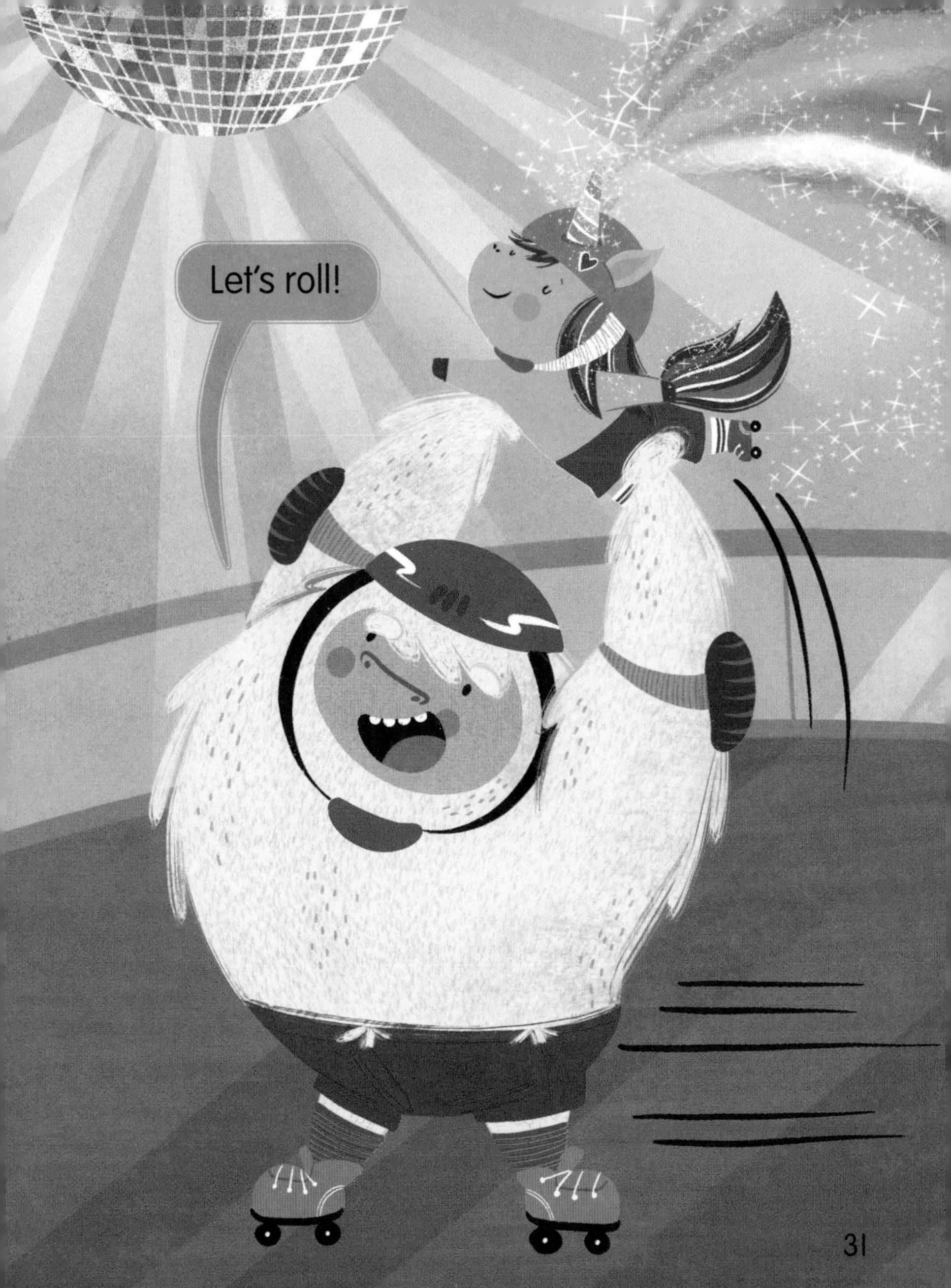
Let's roll!

Chew! Chew! Chew!

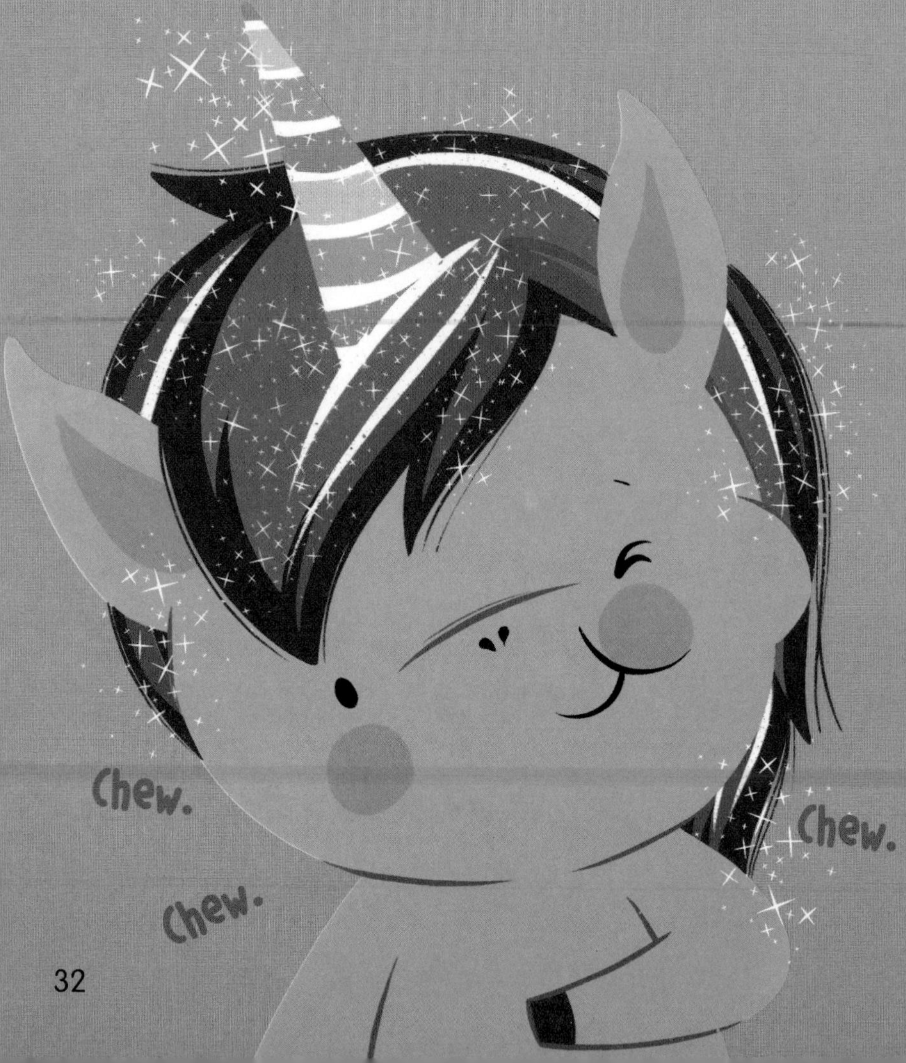
Chew.
Chew.
Chew.

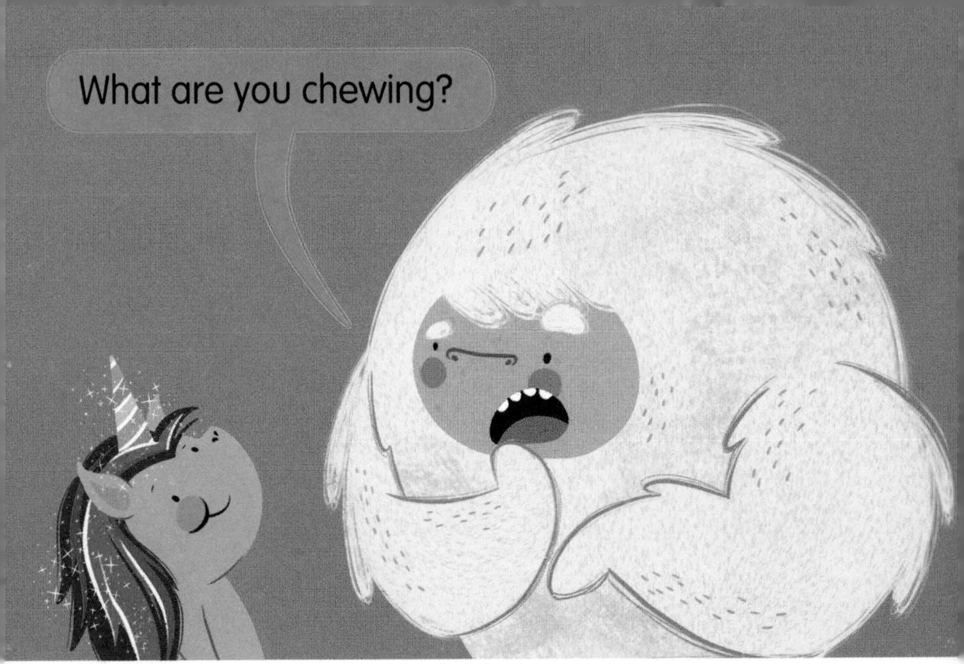
What are you chewing?

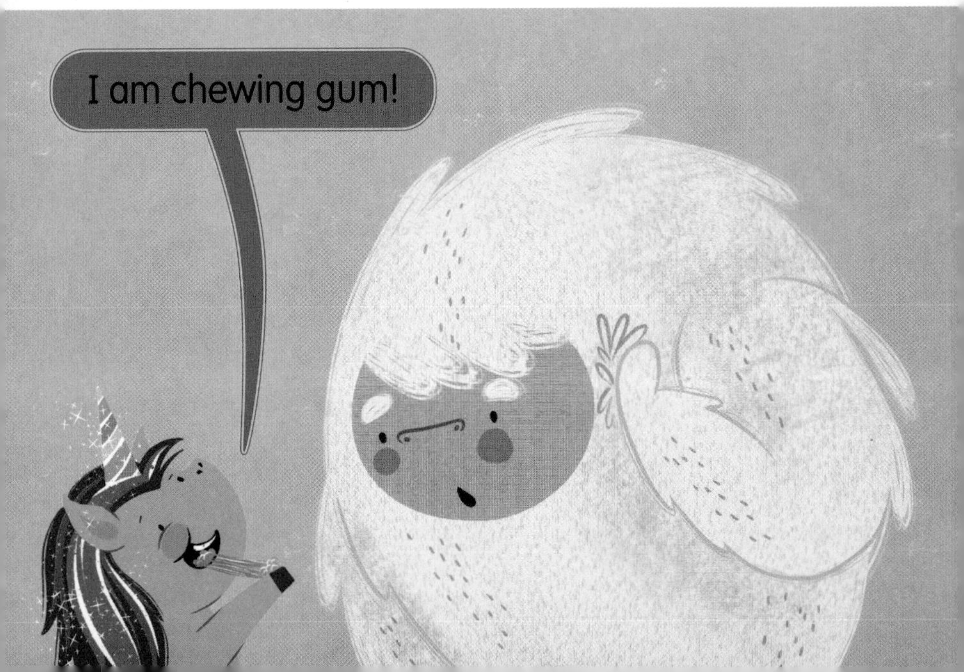
I am chewing gum!

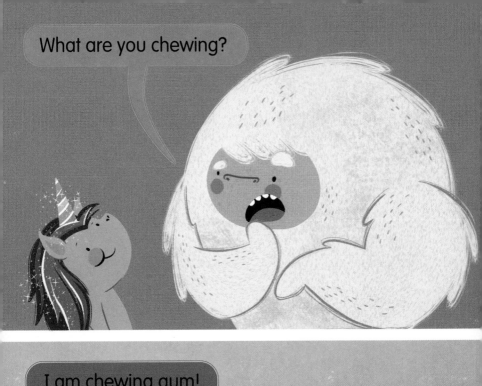

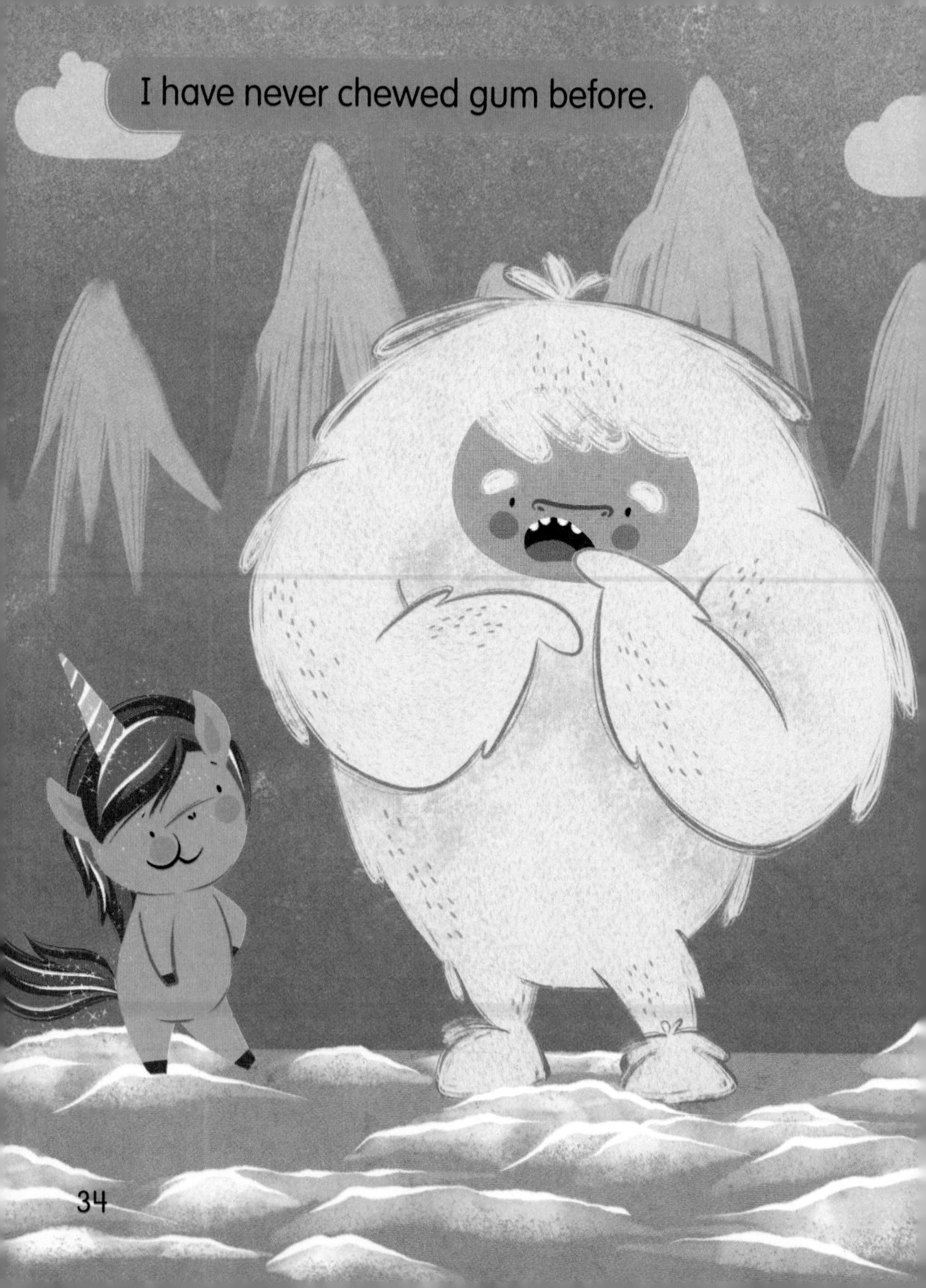
I have never chewed gum before.

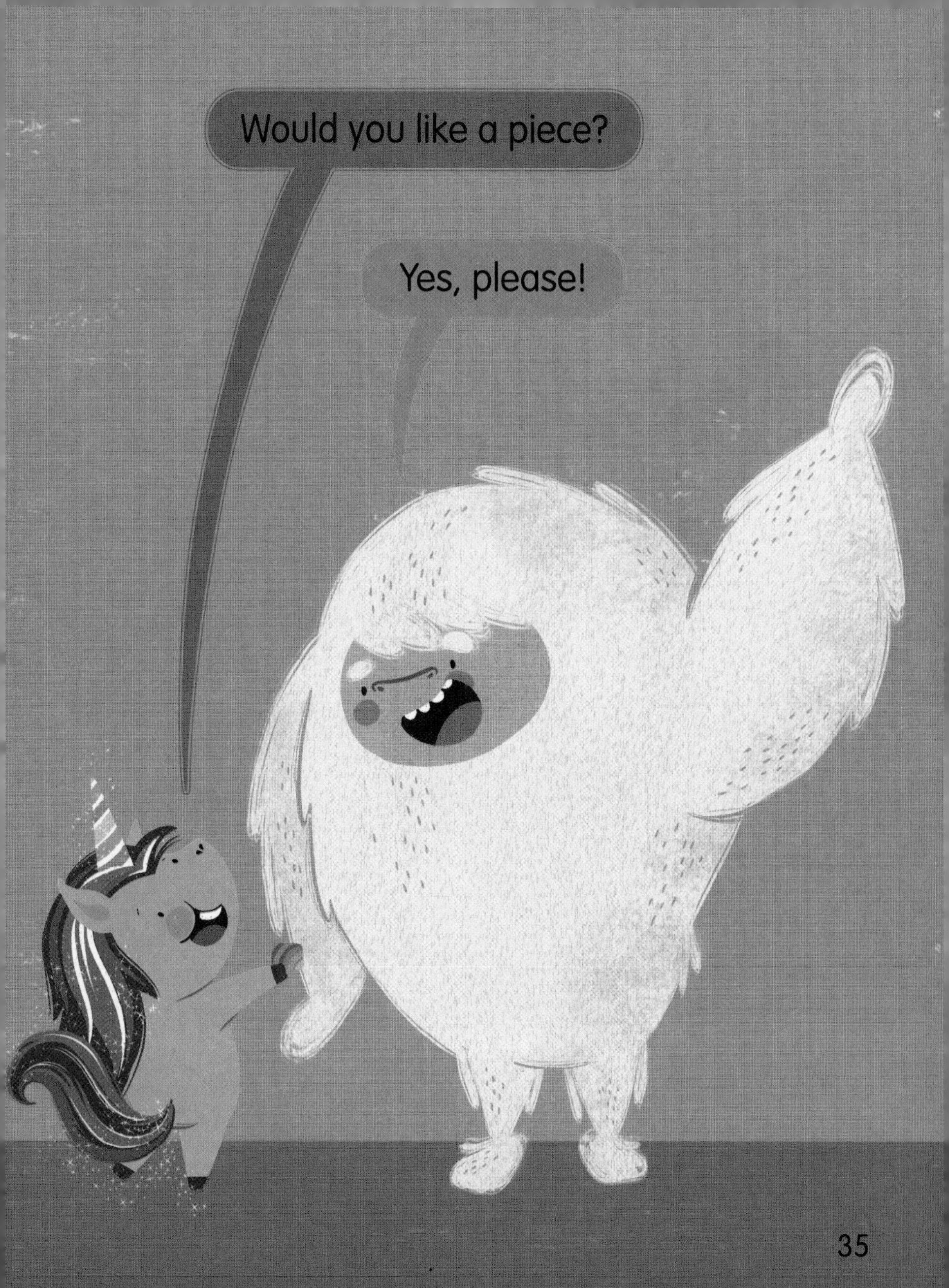
Would you like a piece?
Yes, please!

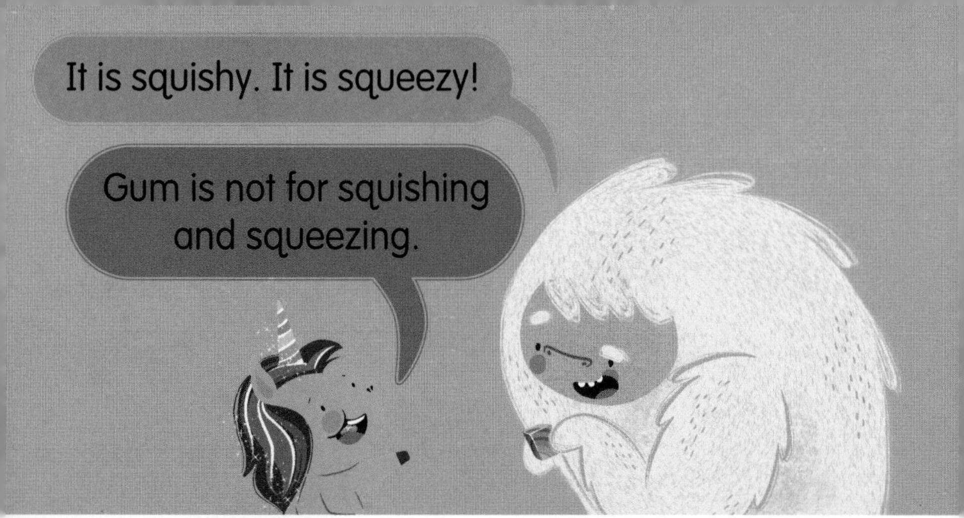
It is squishy. It is squeezy!
Gum is not for squishing and squeezing.

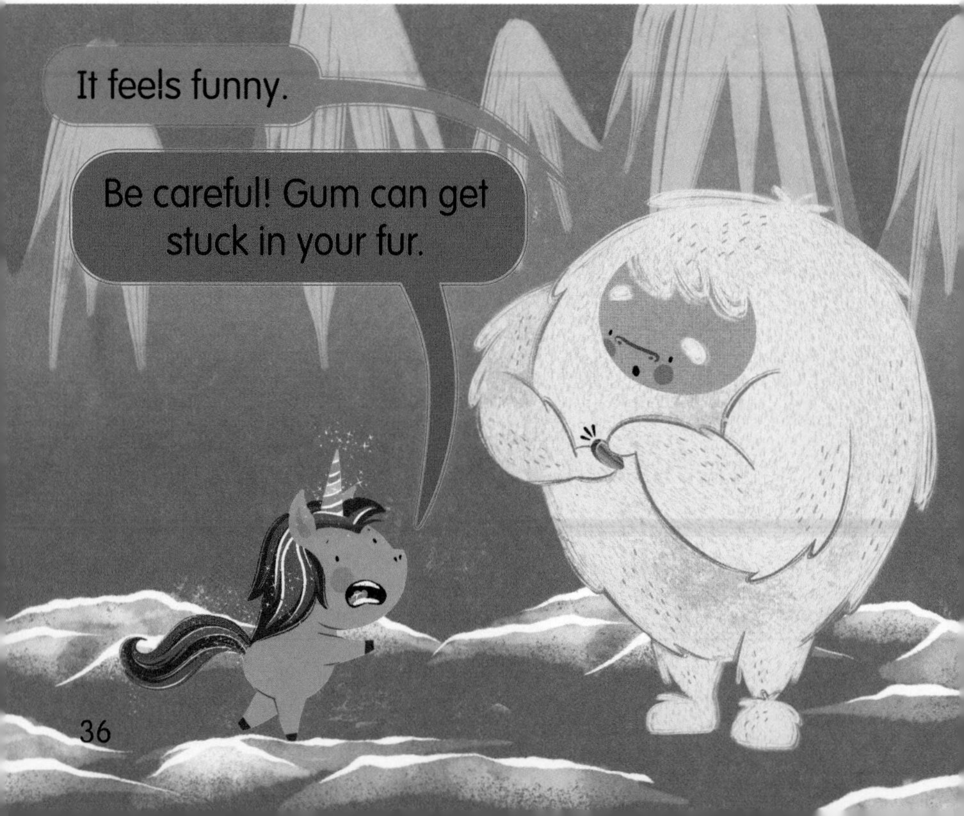
It feels funny.
Be careful! Gum can get stuck in your fur.

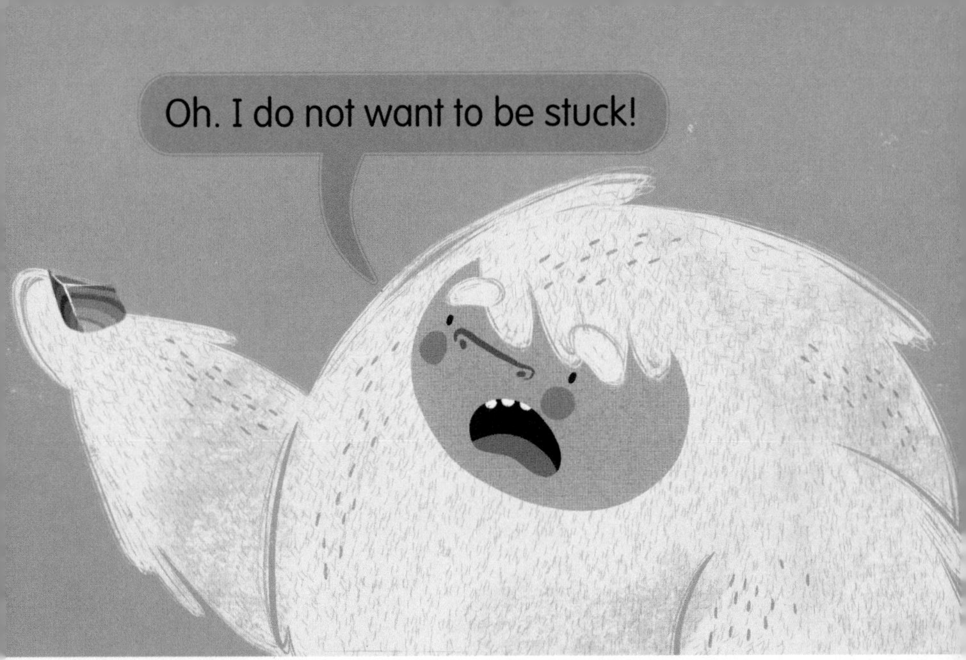
Oh. I do not want to be stuck!

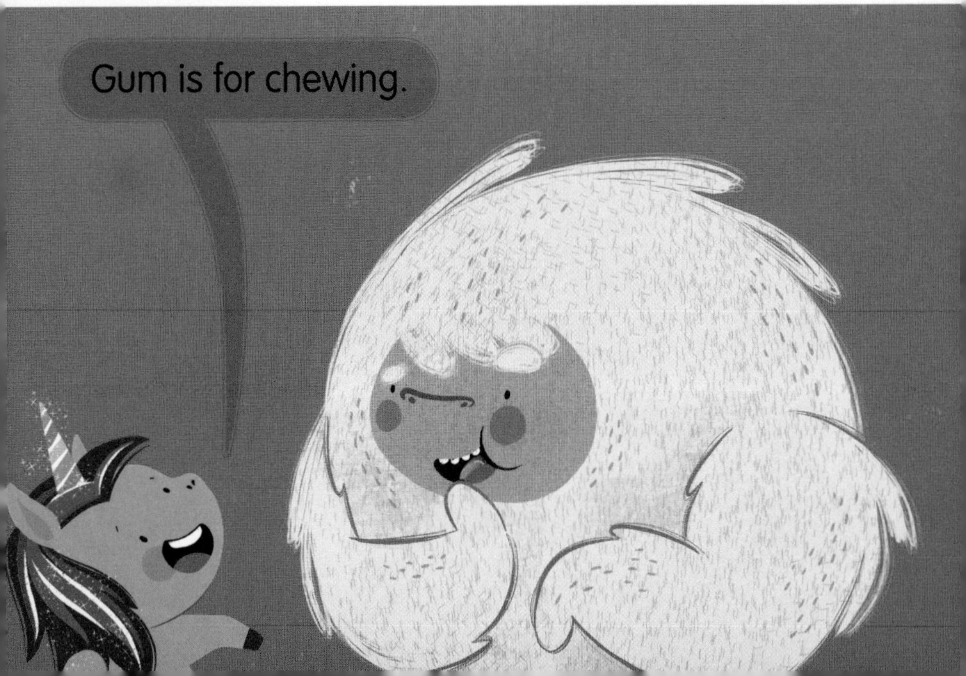
Gum is for chewing.

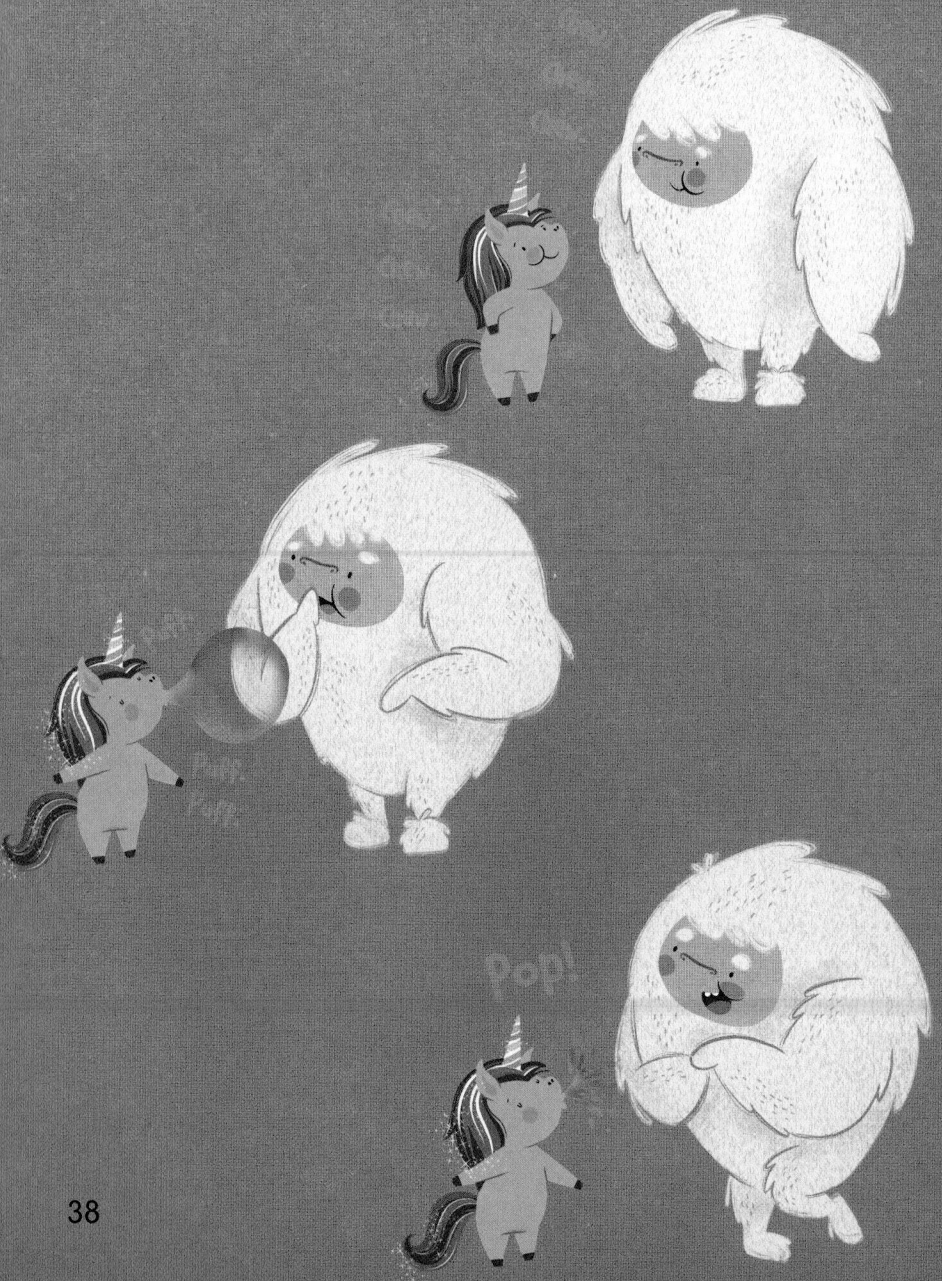
Chew
Chew
Puff.
Puff.
Pop!

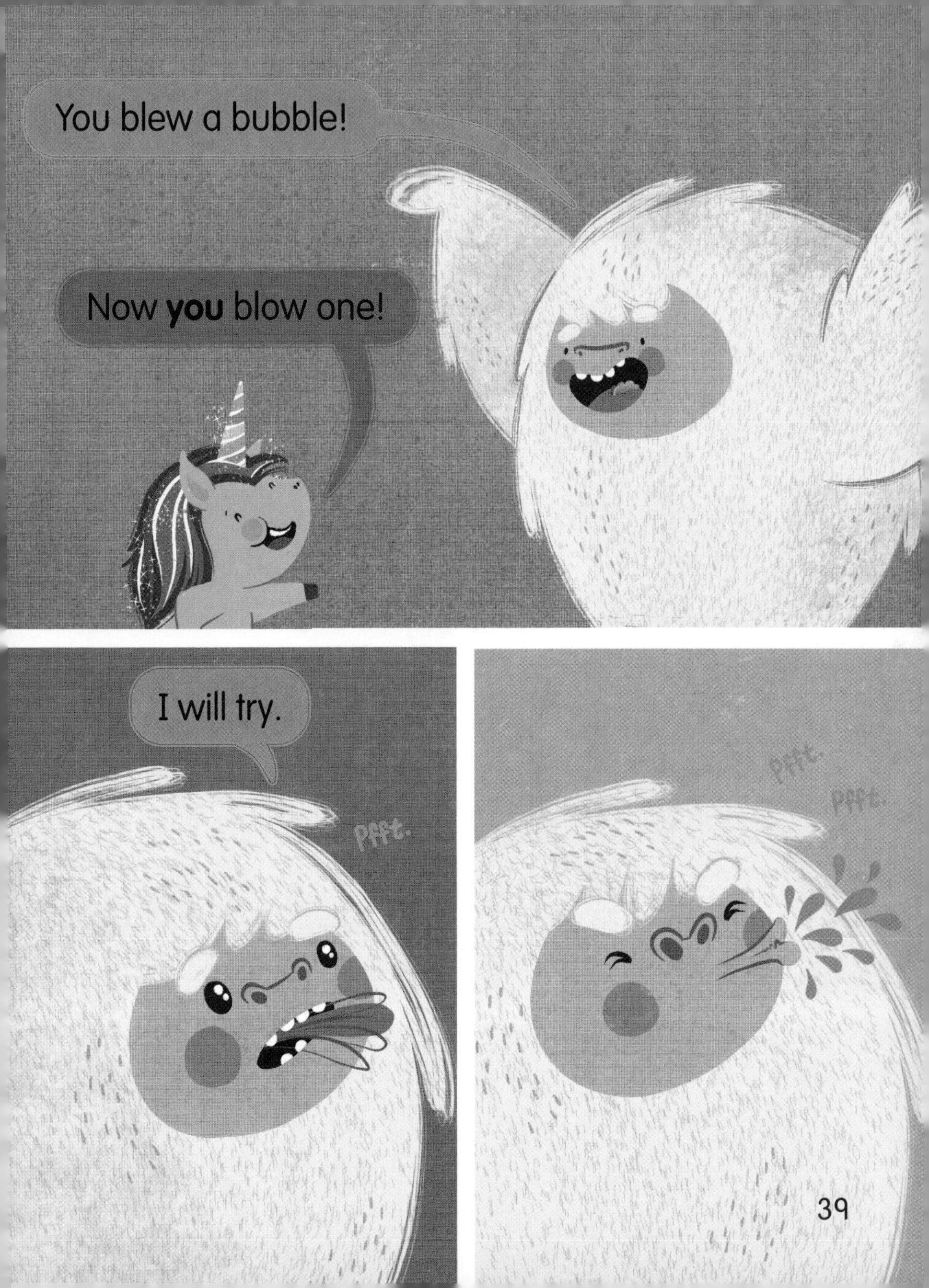
You blew a bubble!
Now **you** blow one!
I will try.
Pfft.
Pfft.
Pfft.

Blowing a bubble is not easy.
Keep trying!
Puff.
Puff.

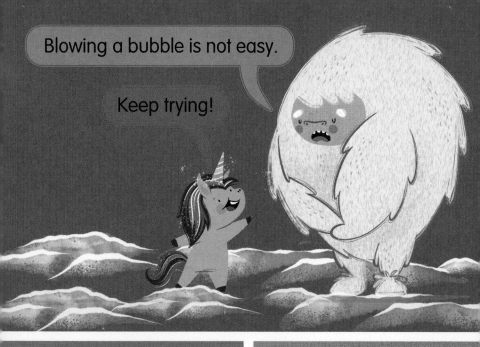

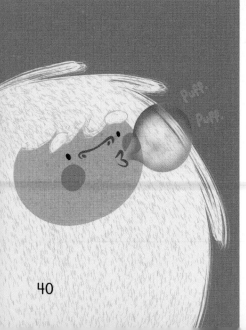

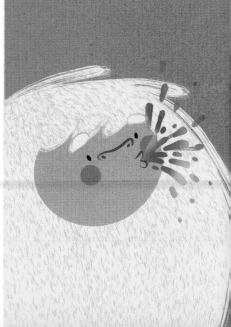

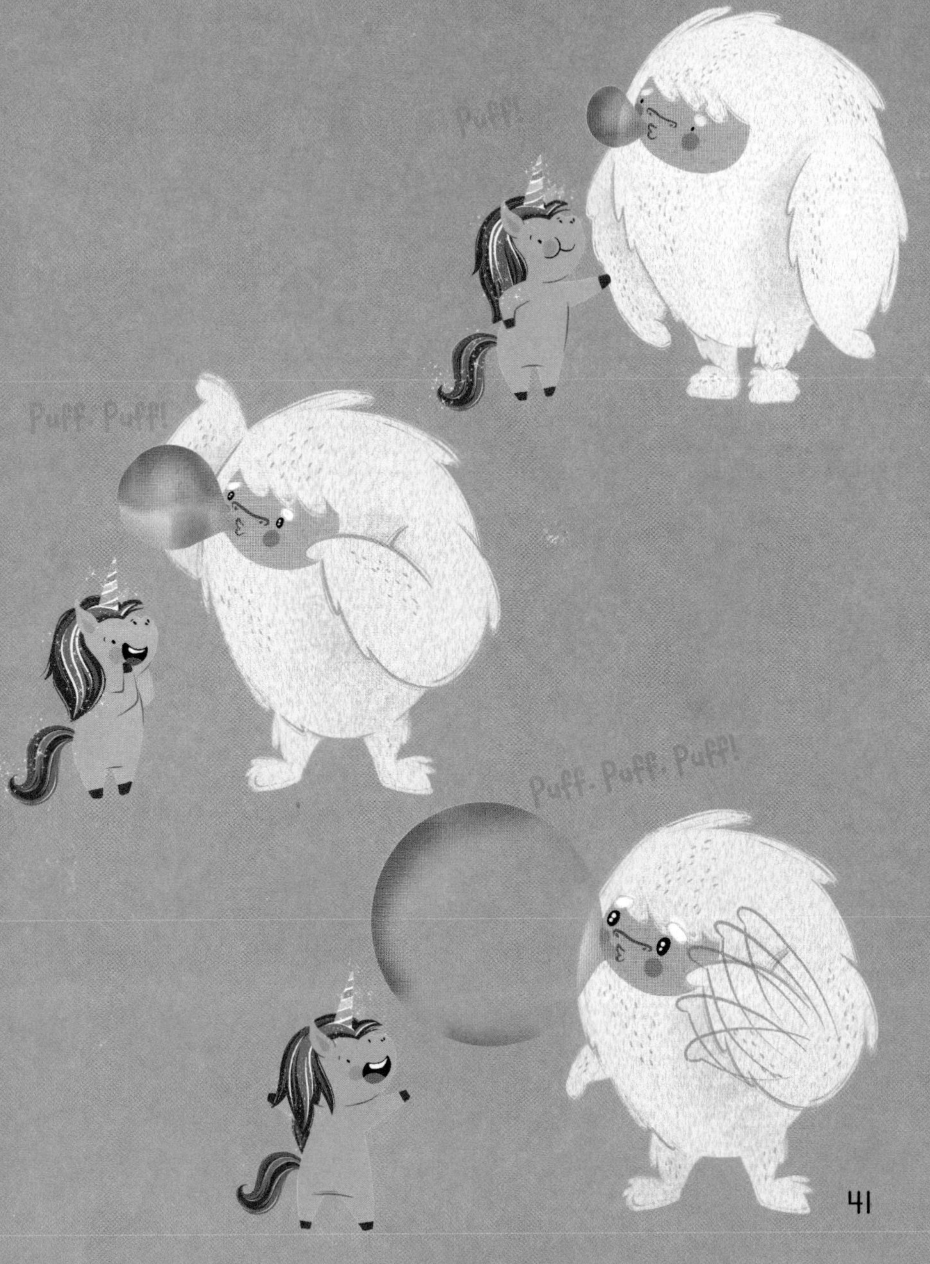
Puff!
Puff, Puff!
Puff, Puff, Puff!

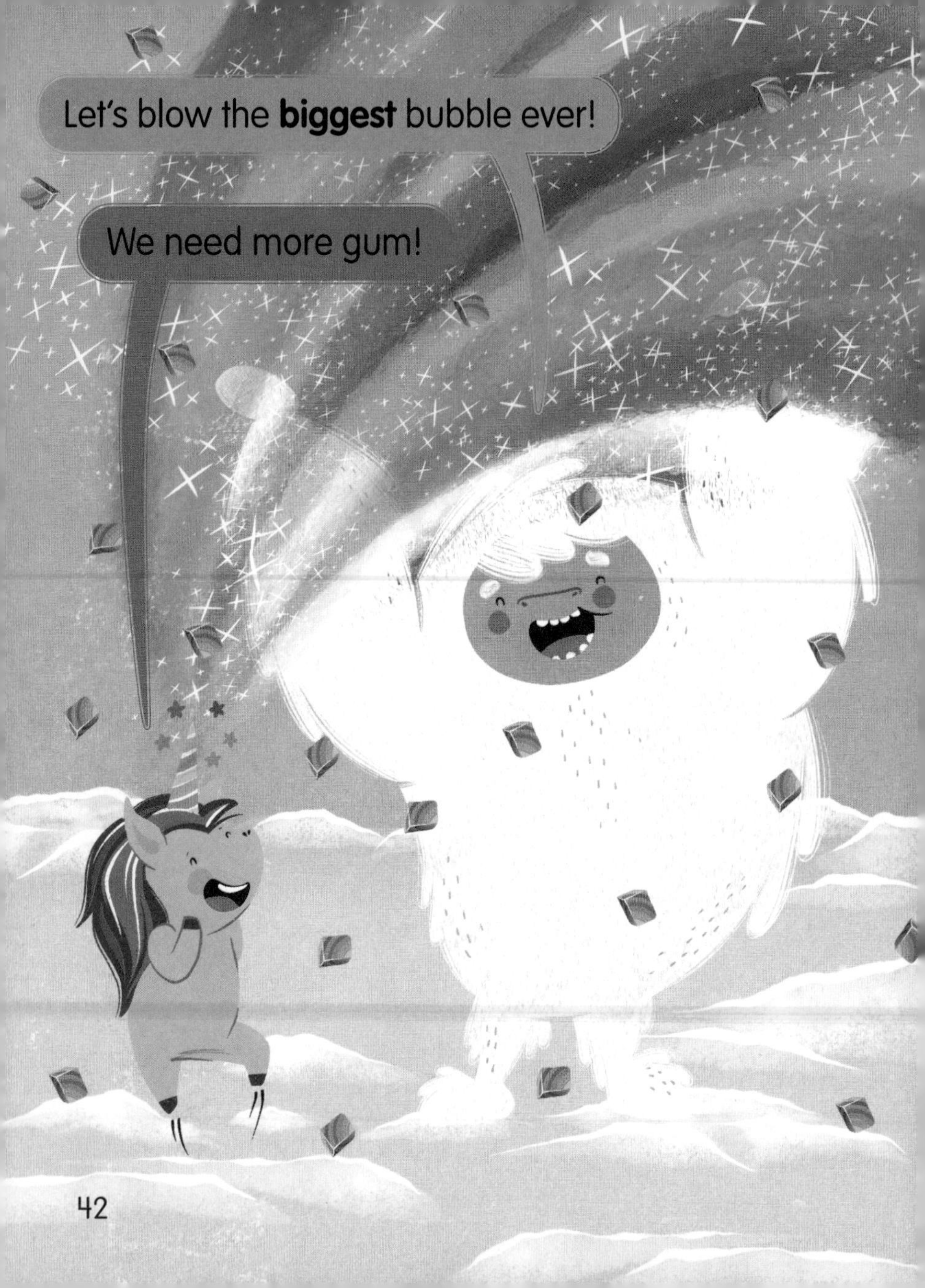
Let's blow the **biggest** bubble ever!
We need more gum!

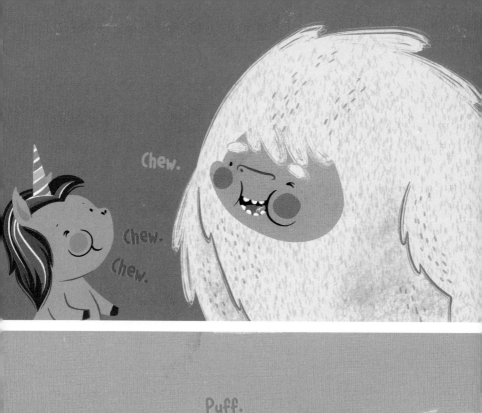

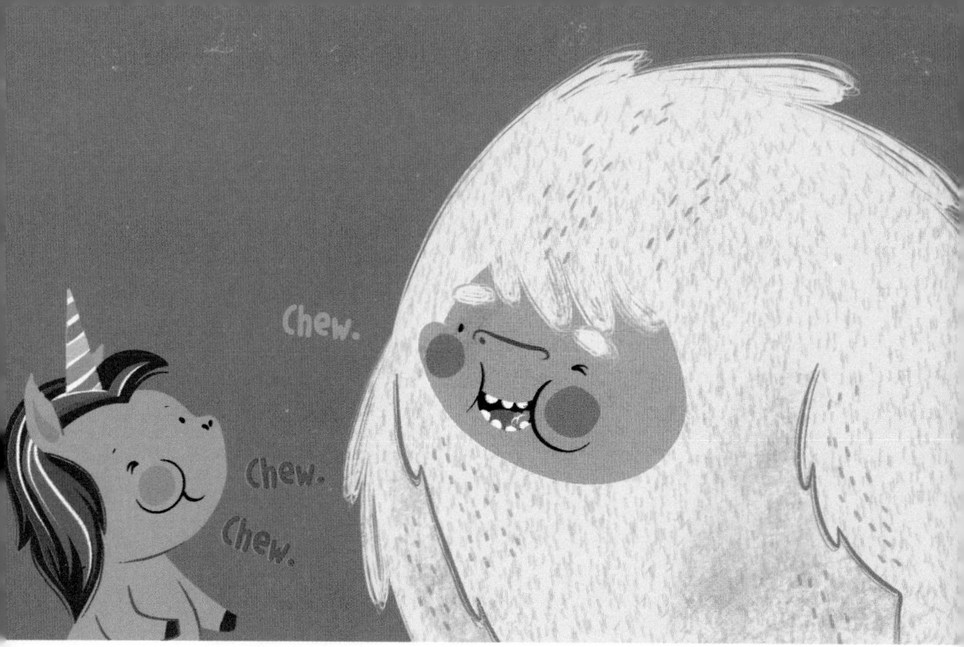
Chew.
Chew.
Chew.

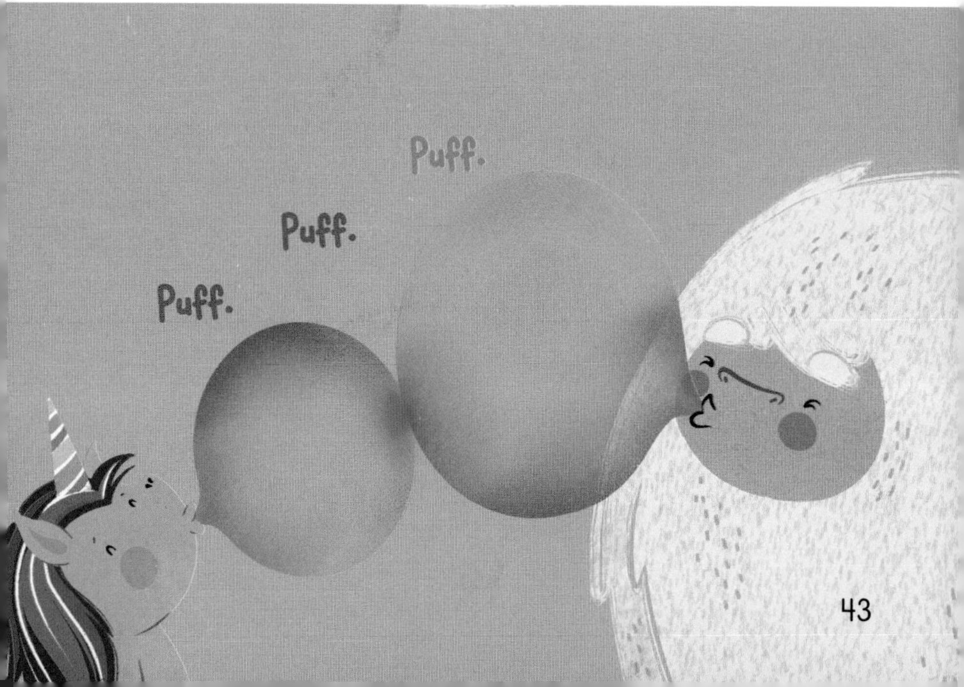
Puff.
Puff.
Puff.

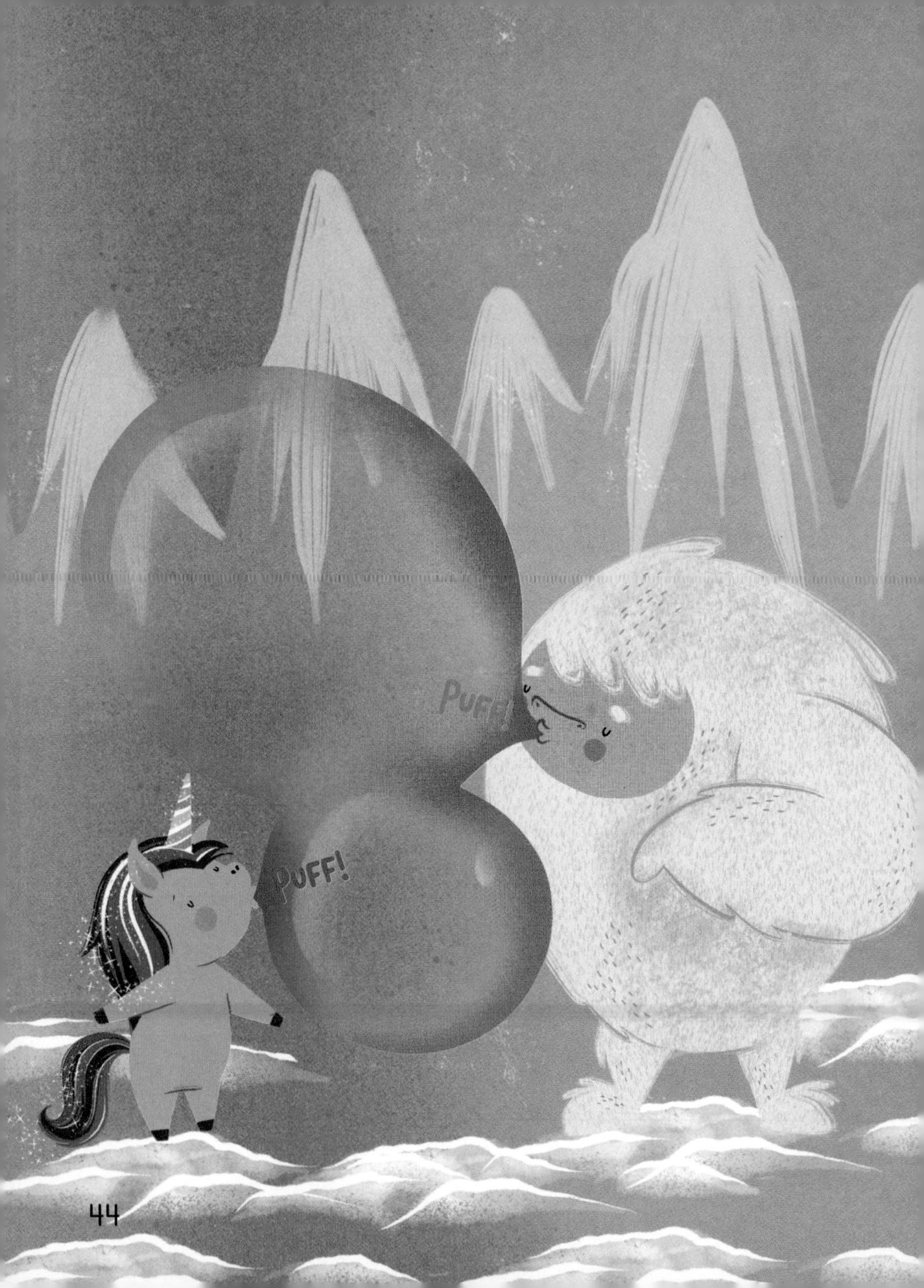
PUFF!
PUFF!

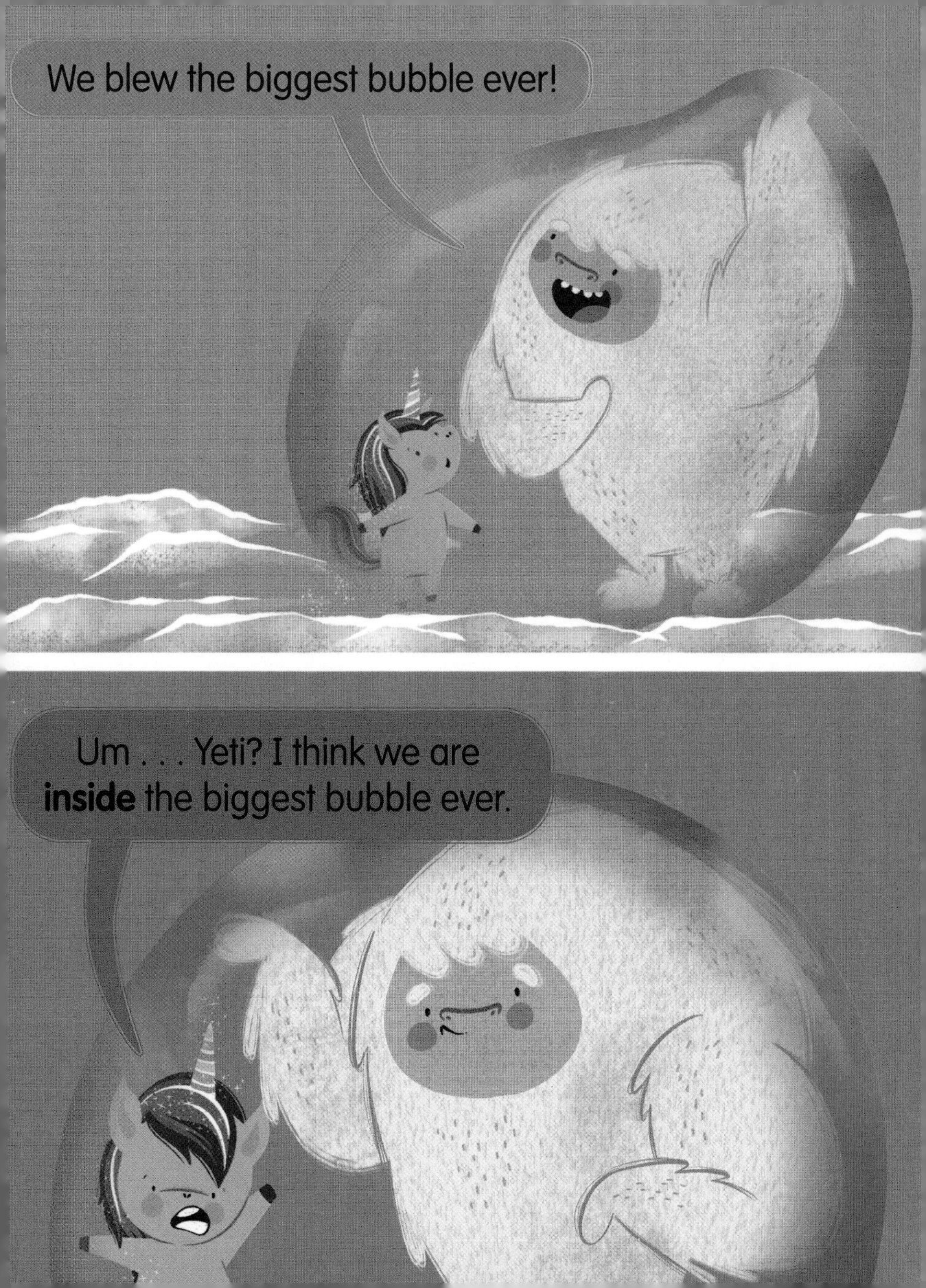
We blew the biggest bubble ever!
Um . . . Yeti? I think we are **inside** the biggest bubble ever.

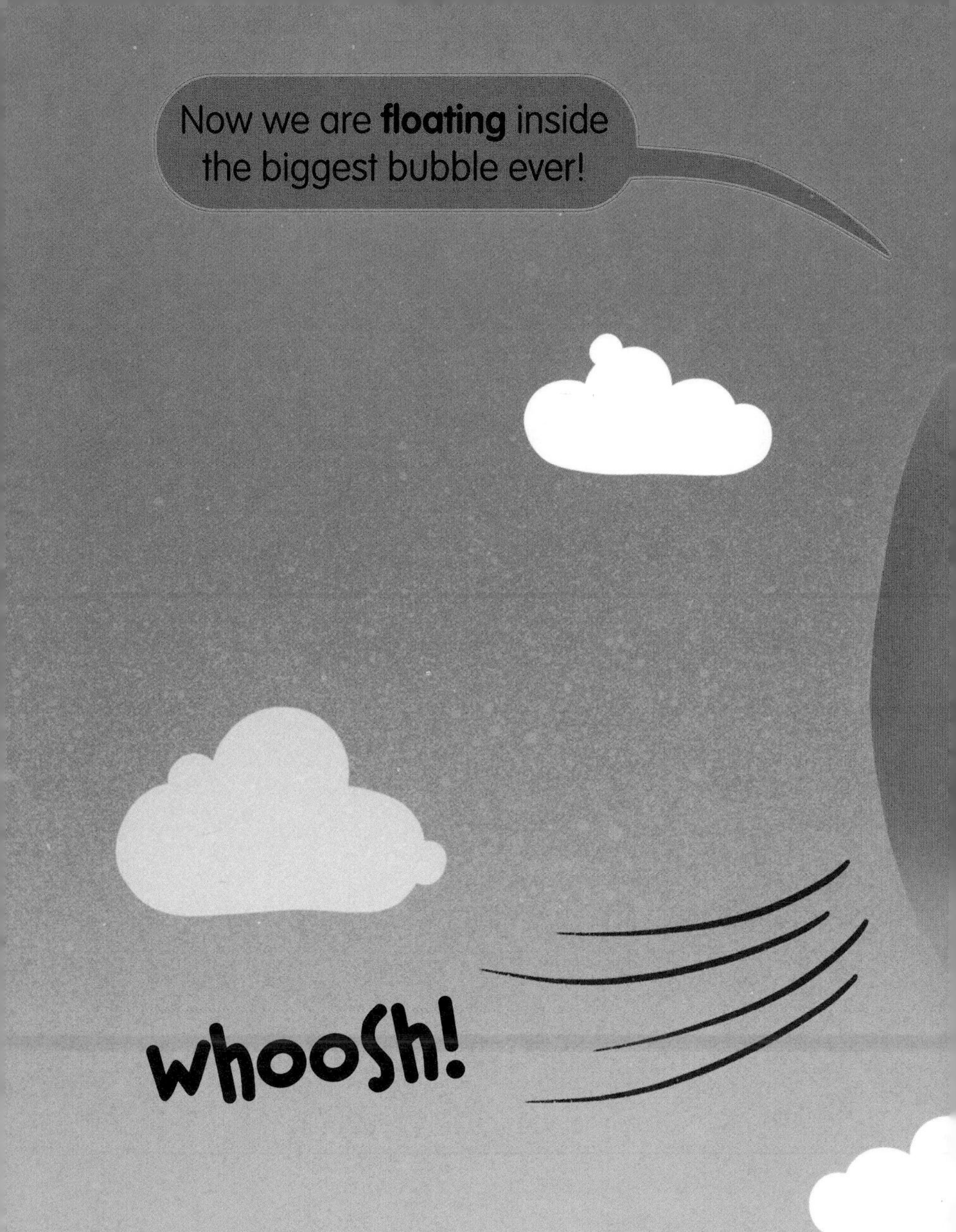
Now we are **floating** inside the biggest bubble ever!
Whoosh!

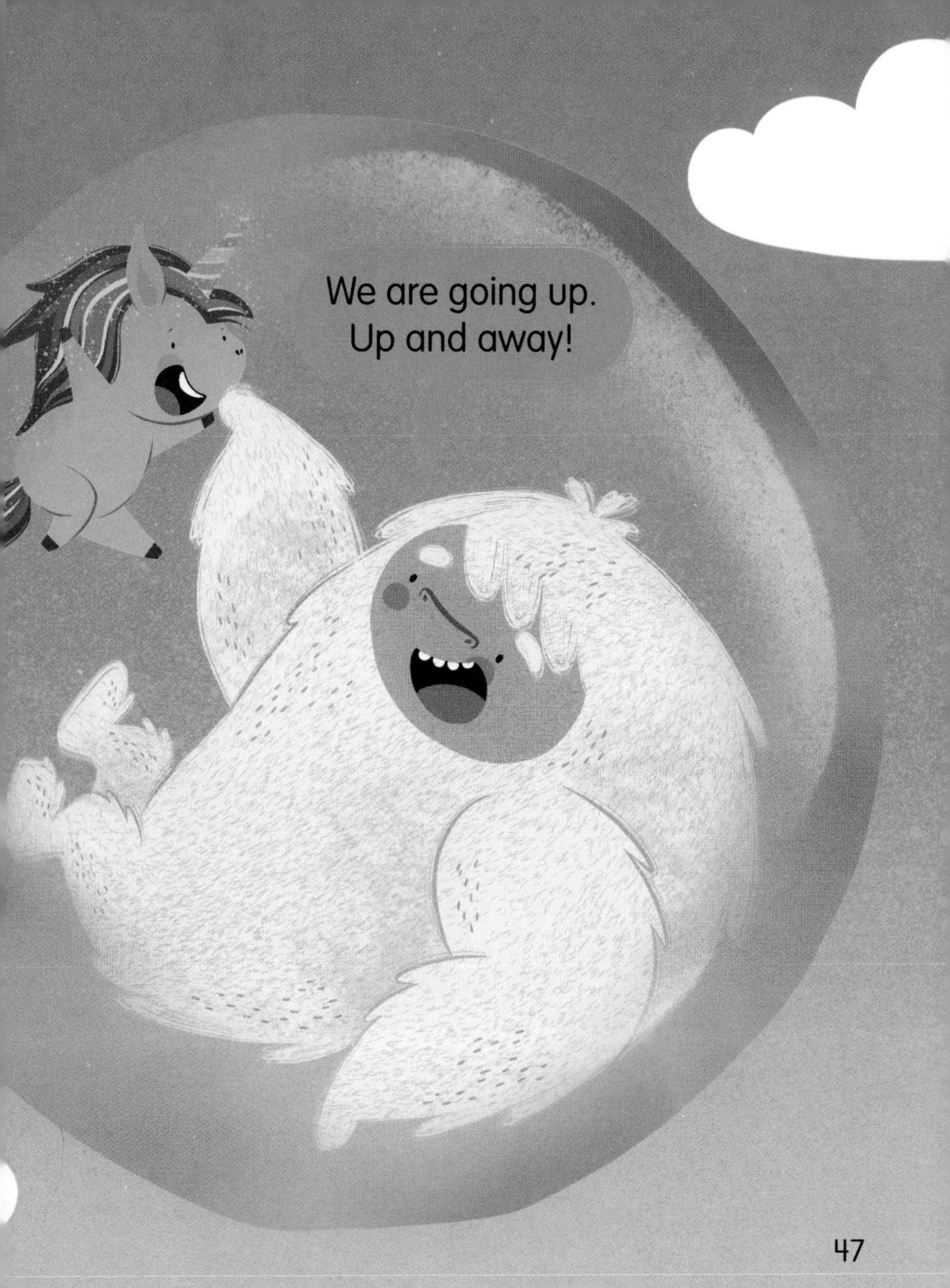
We are going up.
Up and away!

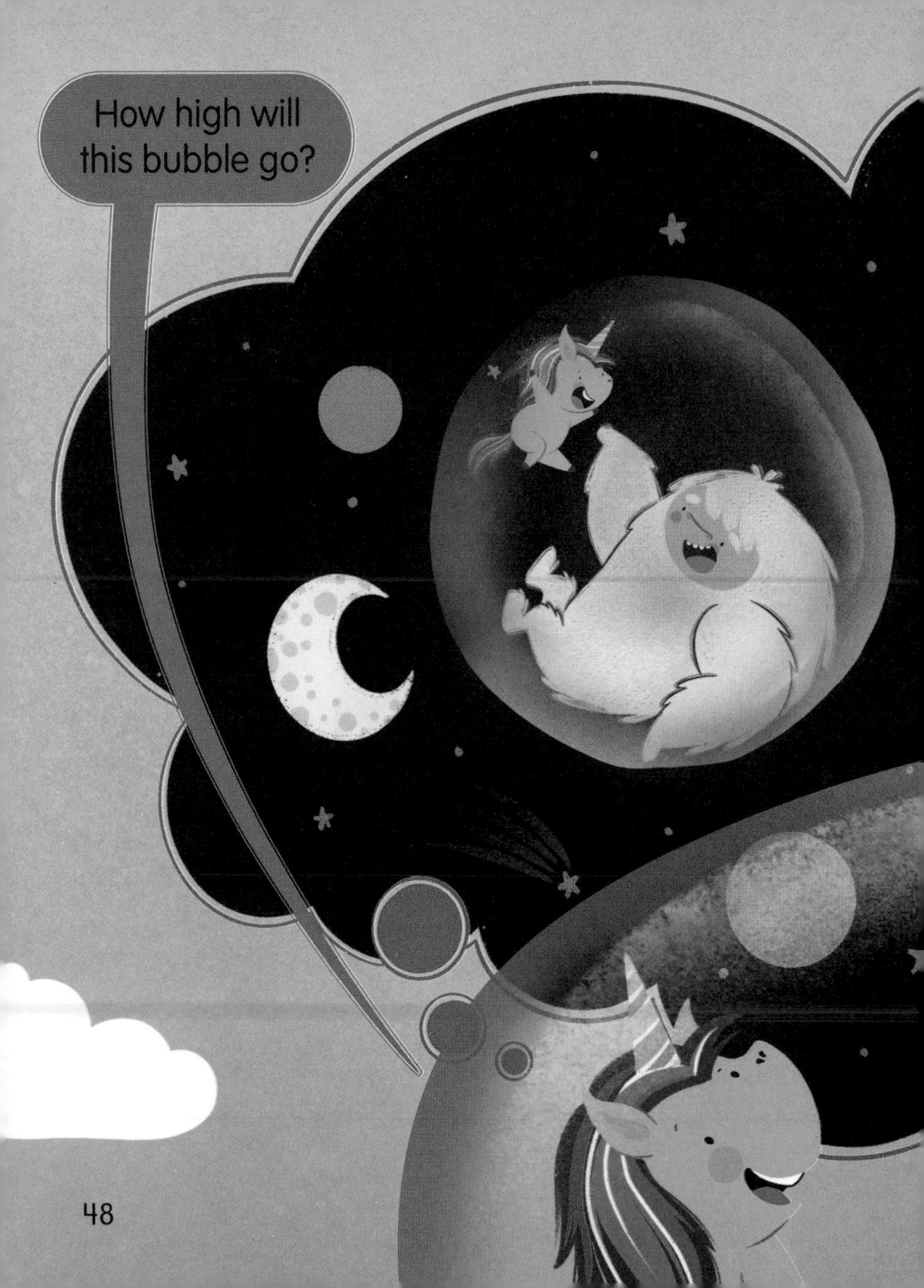
How high will this bubble go?

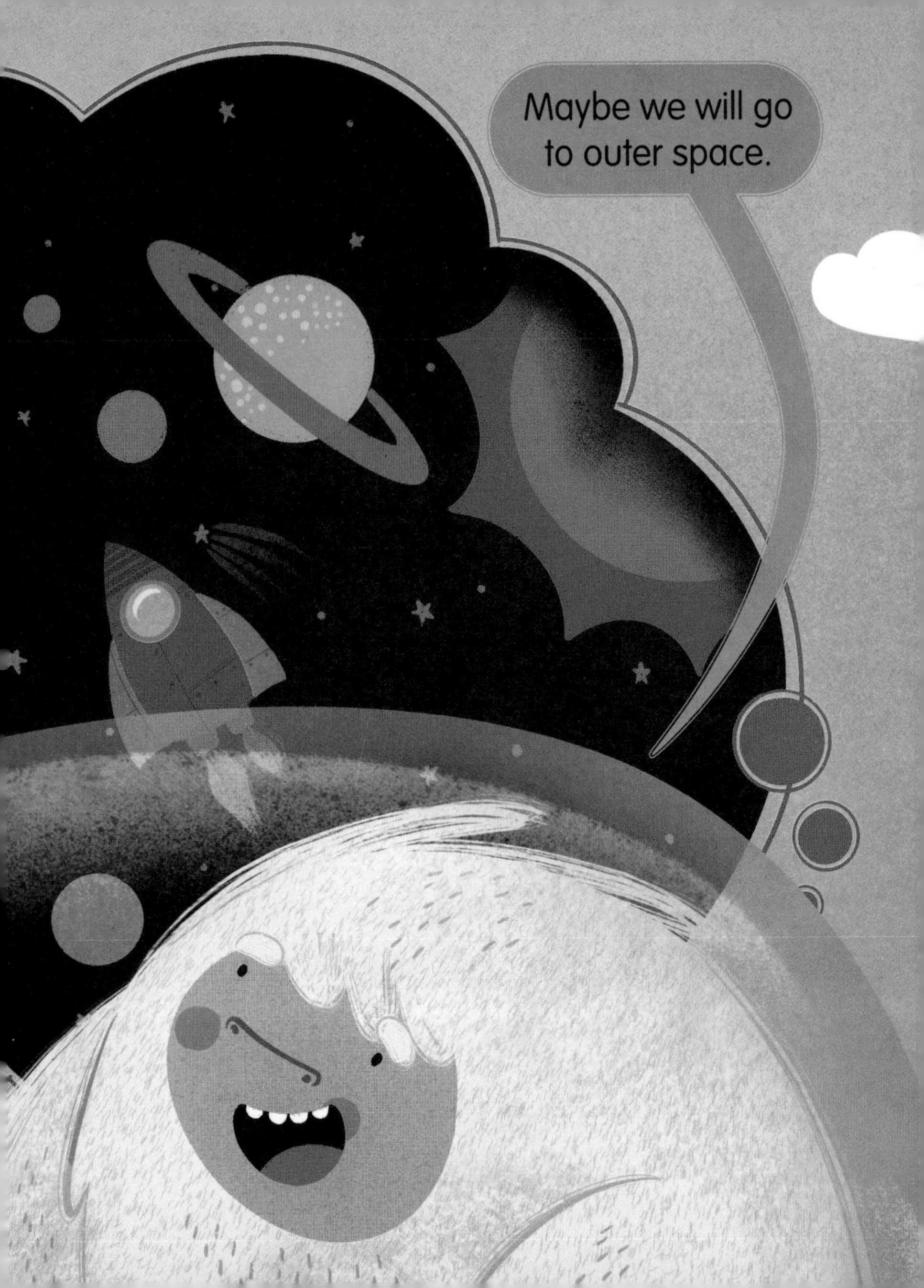
Maybe we will go
to outer space.

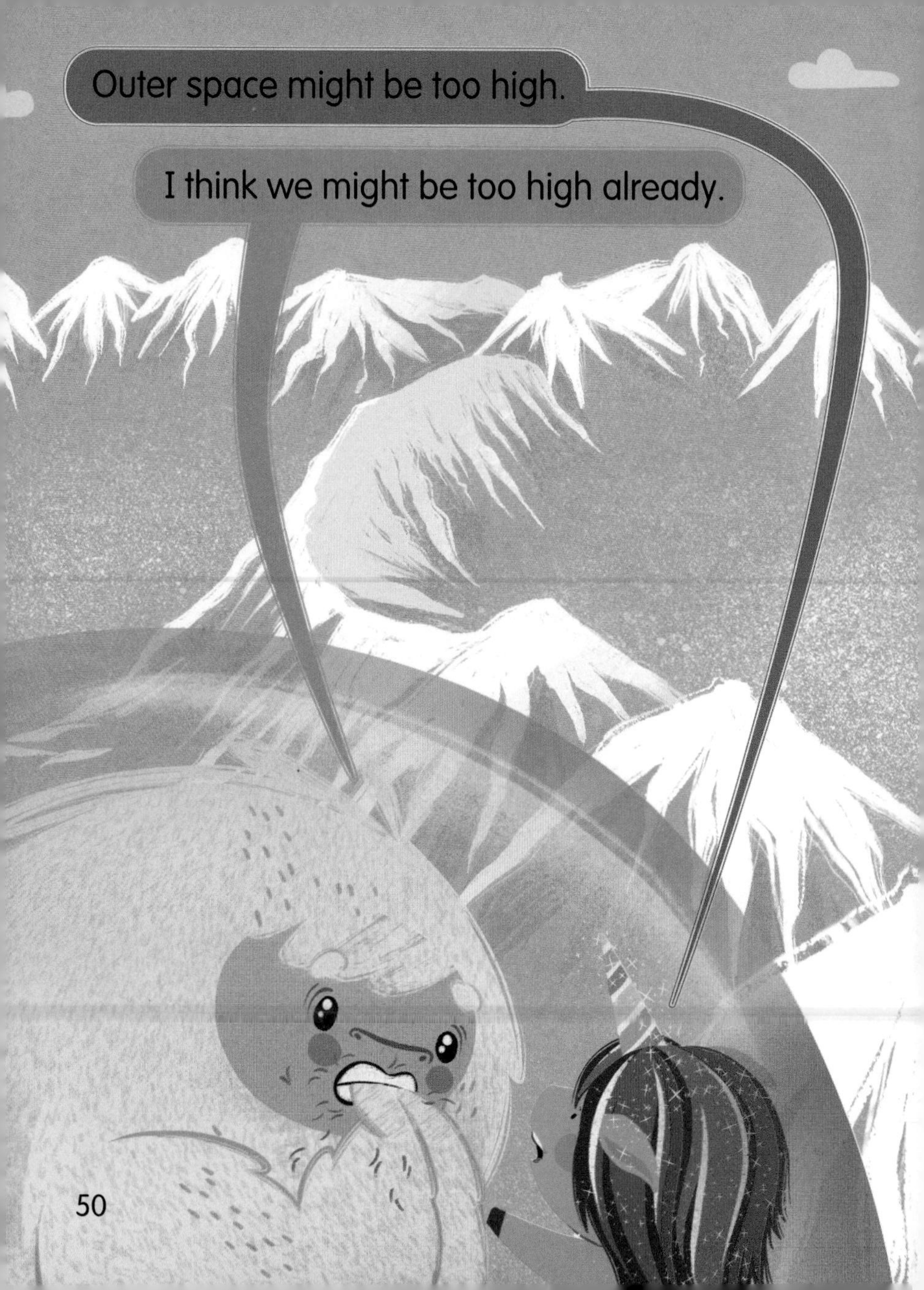
Outer space might be too high.
I think we might be too high already.

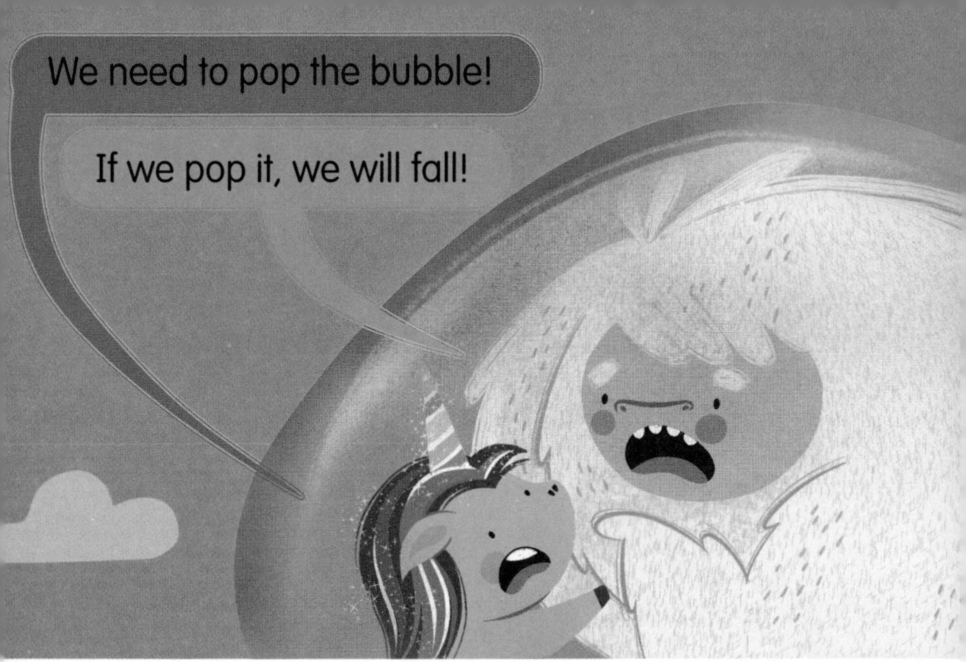
We need to pop the bubble!
If we pop it, we will fall!

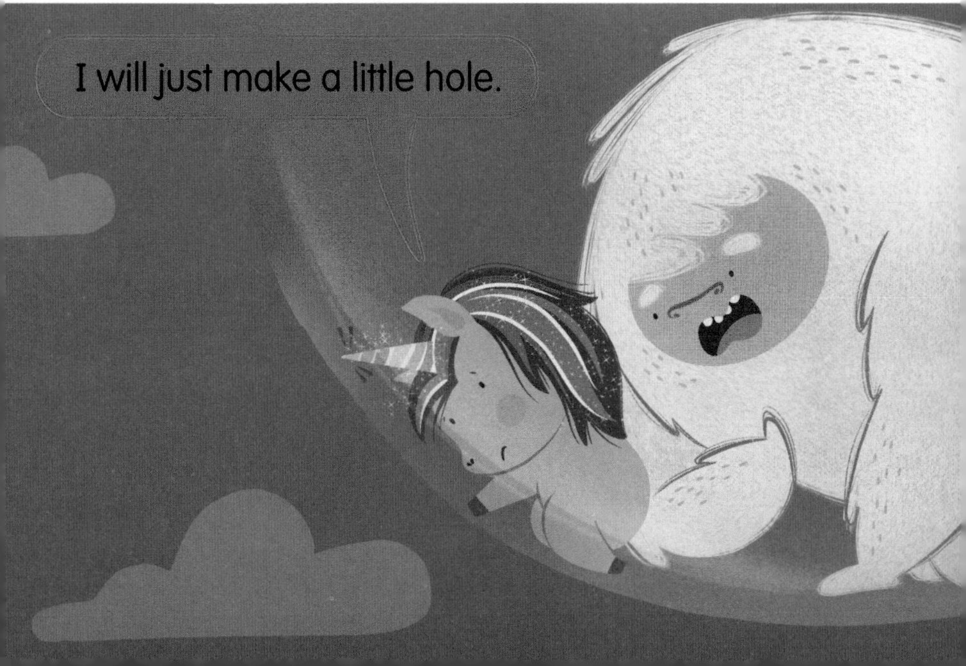
I will just make a little hole.

We are going down!

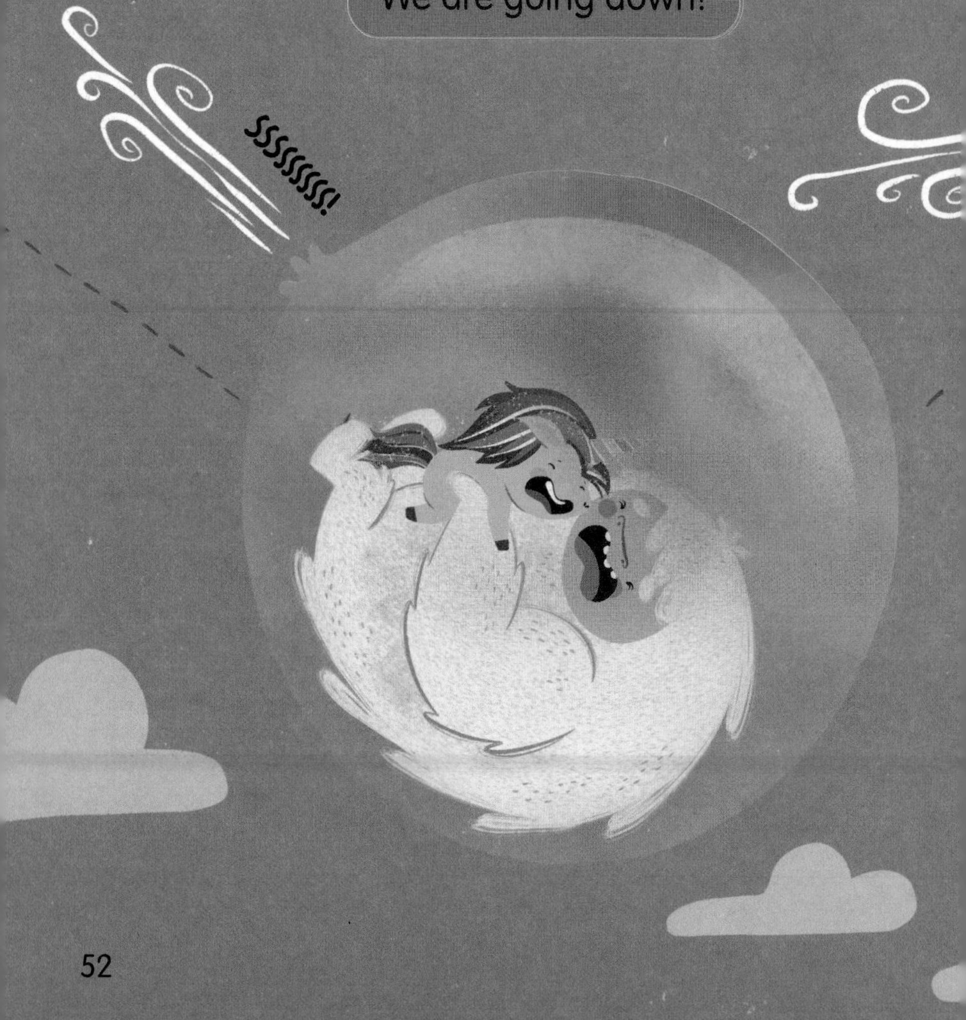
sssssssss!

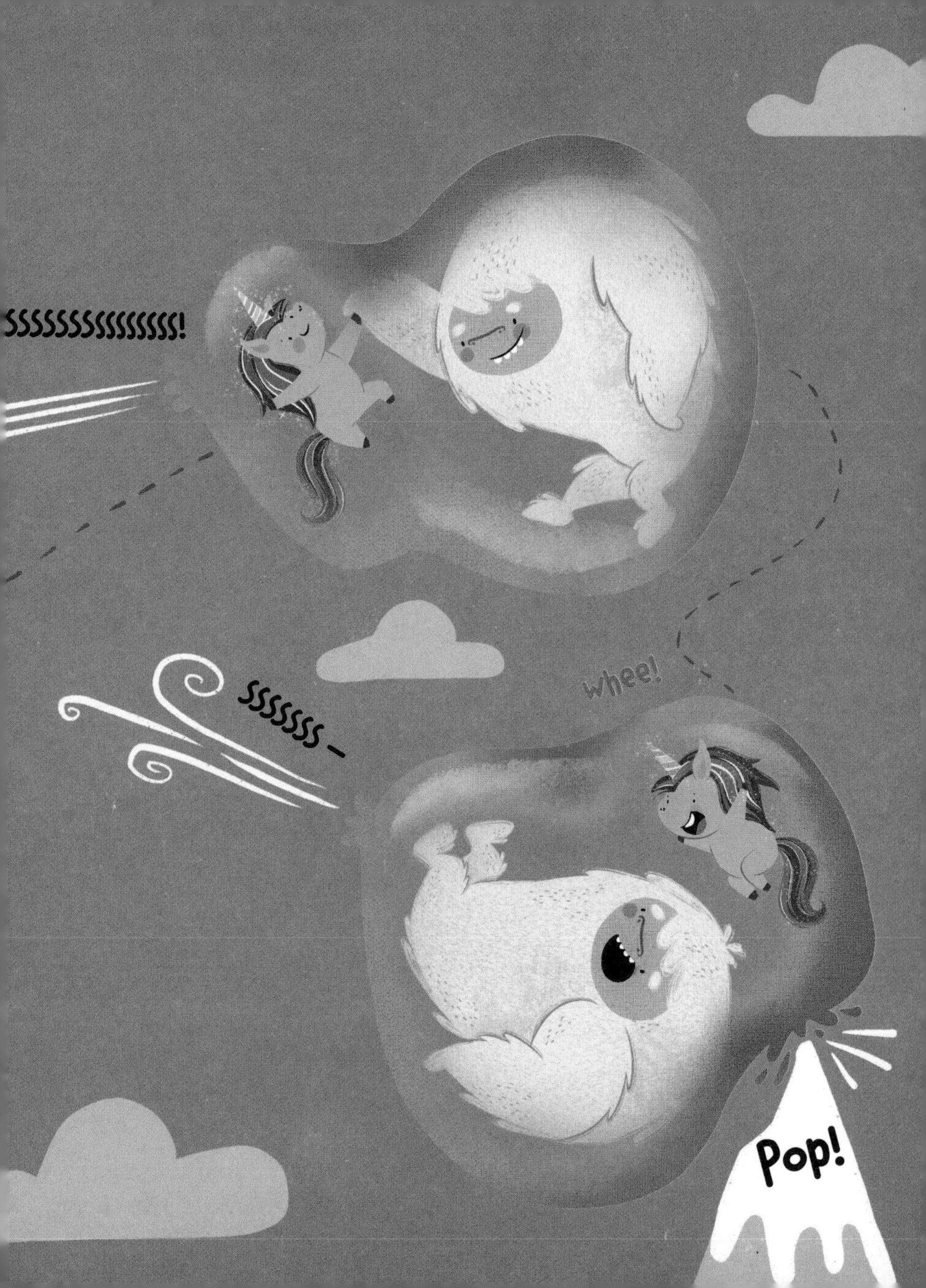
SSSSSSSSSSSSSSSS!
SSSSSSS–
whee!
Pop!

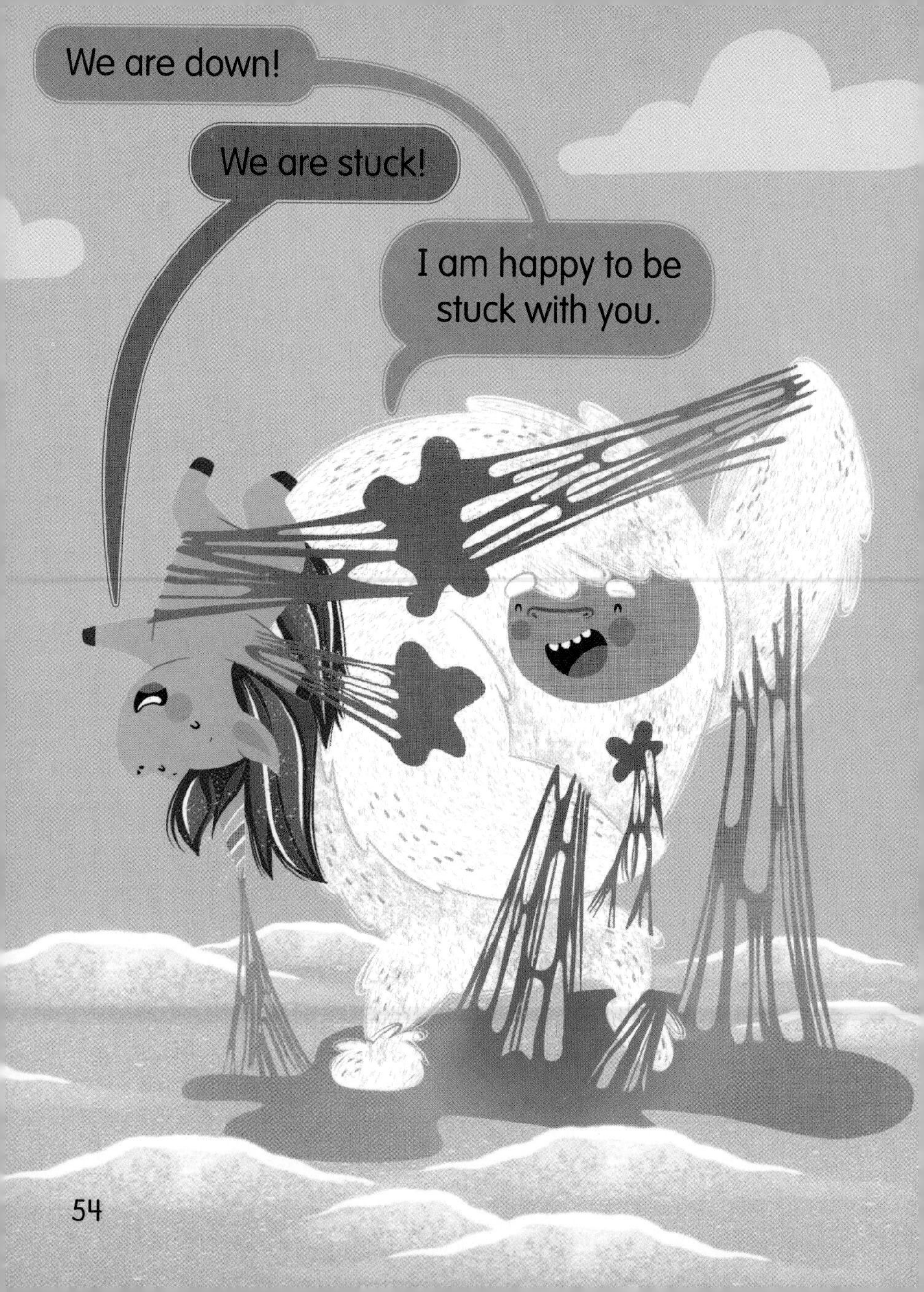
We are down!
We are stuck!
I am happy to be stuck with you.

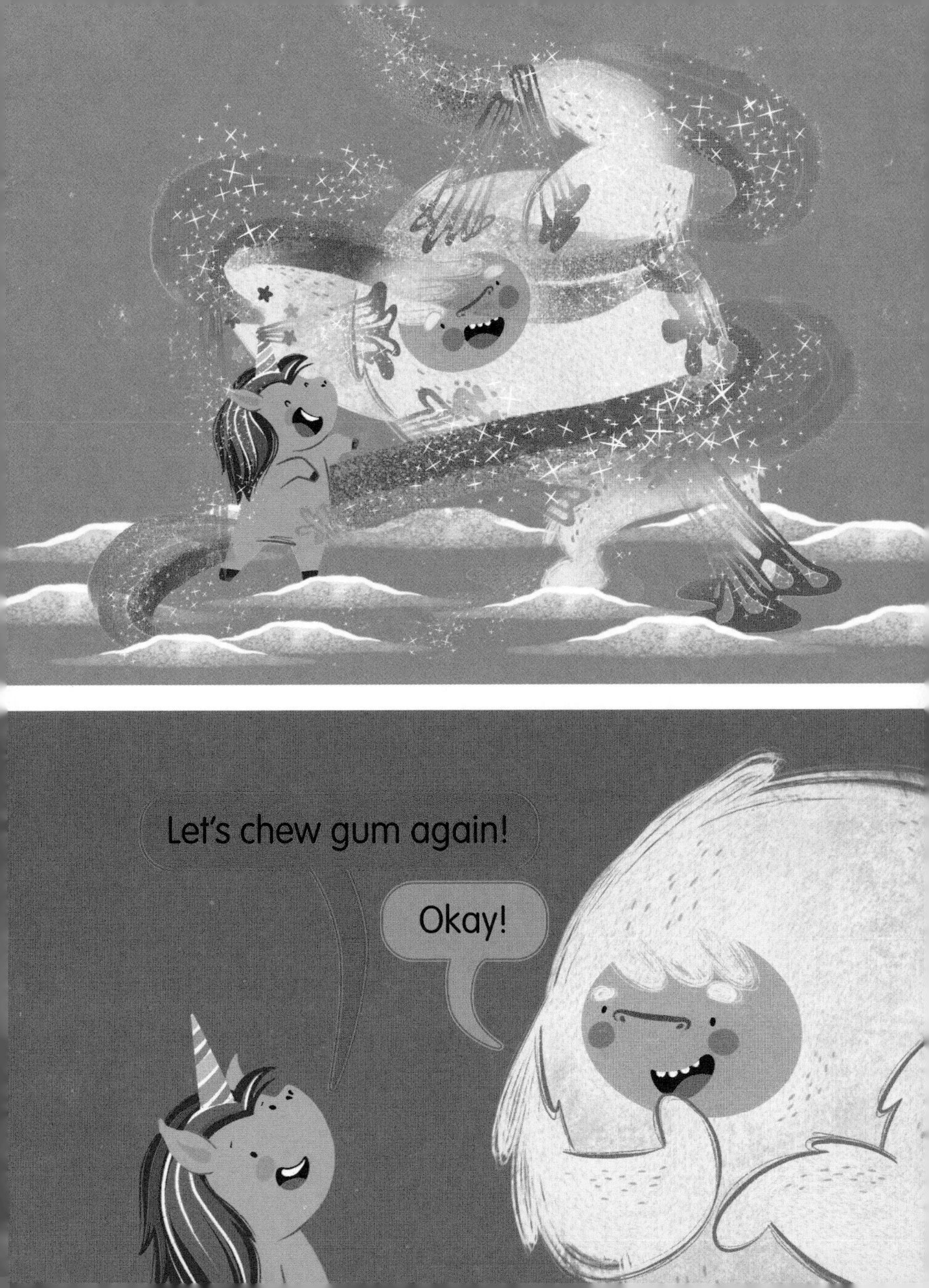
Let's chew gum again!
Okay!

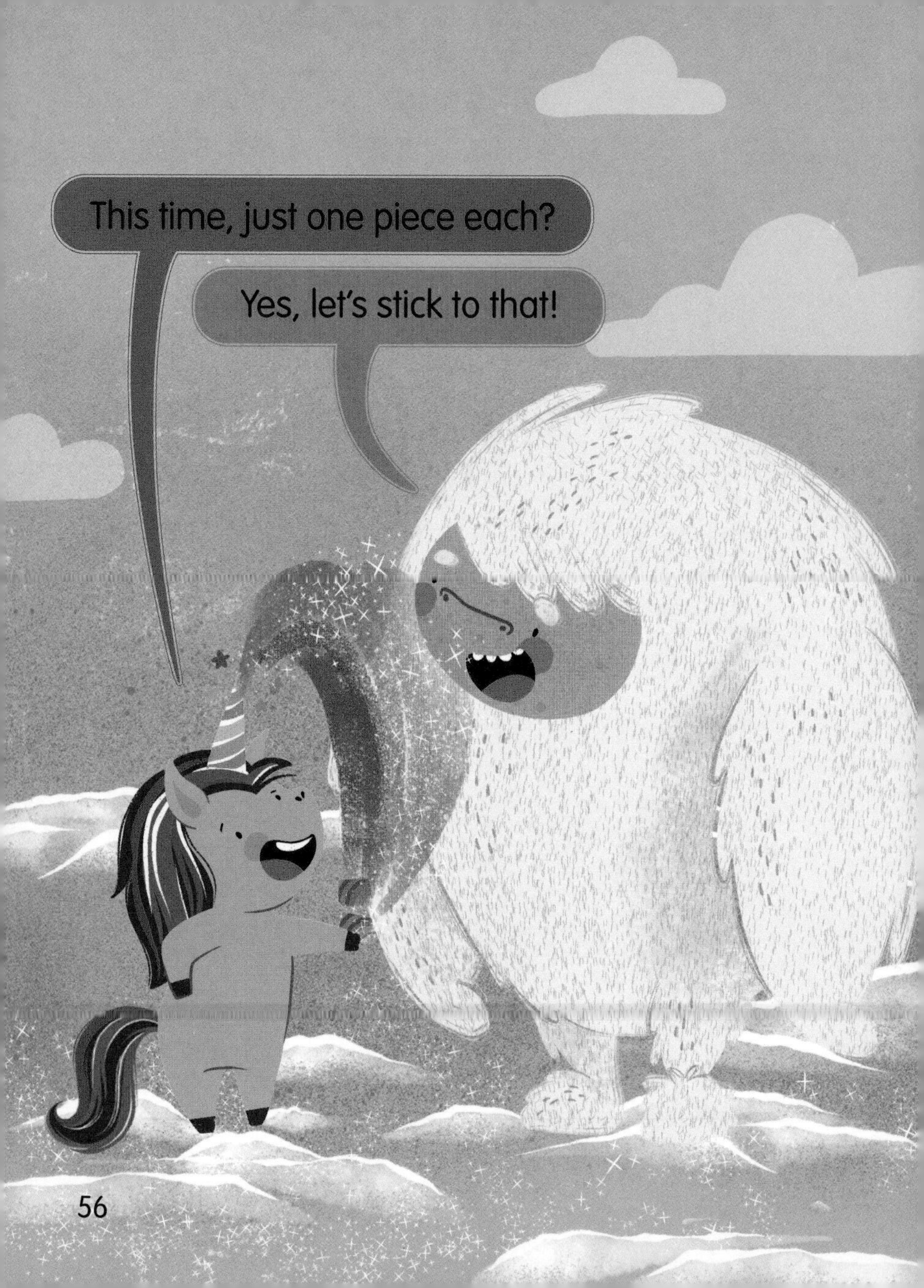
This time, just one piece each?
Yes, let's stick to that!

About the Creators

Heather Ayris Burnell thinks sticking stickers is very fun. She loves to roller-skate, especially when she can go fast. And she likes to blow bubblegum bubbles, even if she has never blown one big enough to make her fly up into

the sky. Heather is a librarian in Washington State, and she is the author of the Unicorn and Yeti early reader series.

Hazel Quintanilla lives in Guatemala. Hazel always knew she wanted to be an artist. When she was a kid, she carried a pencil and a notebook everywhere.

Hazel illustrates children's books, magazines, and games! And she has a secret: Unicorn and Yeti remind Hazel of her sister and brother. Her siblings are silly, funny, and quirky — just like Unicorn and Yeti!

YOU CAN DRAW RAINBOW BUBBLEGUM!

1 Draw three squares. Space them out so you have room to add on to each of them.

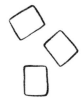

2 On each square, draw three short, straight lines coming out from three corners. Then connect the short lines.

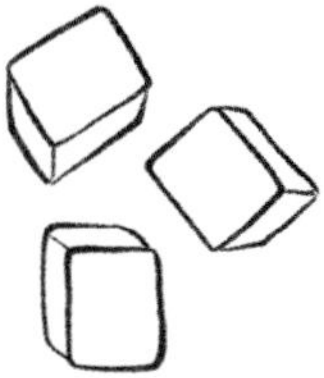

3 On the big side of each square, draw two arched lines. This creates the rainbow pattern on the gum.

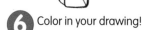

4 Add more arched lines on each of the three squares. Now one side of each gum cube is rainbow-filled!

5 Draw arched lines on the other two sides of each gum cube to make them rainbow-filled, too!

6 Color in your drawing!

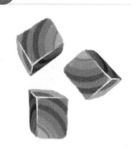

WHAT'S YOUR STORY?

Unicorn and Yeti get stuck inside a big bubble!
Imagine **you** are stuck inside the bubble with them.
What would you see? What would you do?
Write and draw your story!